# THE M〈

# WRETCHED THING

# IMAGINABLE

*or*

## *Beneath the Burnt Umbrella*

# STEPHEN MOLES

Sagging
Meniscus

ISBN: 978-1-944697-15-0 (paperback)
ISBN: 978-1-944697-16-7 (ebook)
Library of Congress Control Number: 2016944017

Sagging Meniscus Press
web: http://www.saggingmeniscus.com/
email: info@saggingmeniscus.com

# Translator's Note

The original and translated versions of this text are one and the same thing. *The Most Wretched Thing Imaginable* was located in a transcrypt of its own contents and was forced, by a metafictional bookworm twist, to turn in its grave an odd number of times so that its about-face would bear witness to an alternative original upon its resurrection.

It was recomposed through the granting of autopoietic license to conceive of itself in the world as a palimpsestuous preparaphrasing of the corpus to which it would later provide essential support as a Siamese limb.

As the body of text shifts its weight from left to right, observing the on- and offbeats of its dual nature, it therefore inscribes a 7/4 spacetime signature at its base, identifying its author as its translator and its beginning as its end. A hole is punched in the page by Odd's bodkin so that the unconscious of literature—symbolism stripped bare by its bachelors, even—can be seen throbbing beneath the book bonnet.

ANY birds, through no fault of their own, are forced to carry terrible secrets around inside them...

A feathered creature can be forced into becoming the custodian of the memory of a dark human deed for the rest of its days simply by being in the wrong place at the wrong time.

A bluebird that builds a nest near a road may find that the sight of a fatal hit-and-run incident becomes a rotten egg that it has to sit on for the rest of its life to stop a plot for revenge being hatched out elsewhere and causing even more lives to be destroyed. While the amnesic driver wakes up the next day with a hangover and experiences mild confusion about why there is a dent in his Volkswagen Beetle, the traumatised bird suffers intense recurring nightmares about the terrible burden it has taken on.

A dove that happens to be sitting on a telegraph wire may glance in the direction of a bedroom window and be left with the knowledge that the upcoming marriage of two humans should not go ahead because the bridegroom has had an illicit liaison with the chief bridesmaid. The poor creature will have to forever hold its peace as the secret pecks away at it from the inside.

Next time you admire the sweet-sounding song of a lark, it is worth remembering that the melody may be the means by which the bird is drowning out the sour notes being played repeatedly in its head because of the selfish actions of someone you know.

The dawn chorus covers the screams from the night before.

HAT can those creatures with their infamously tiny brains teach us?

Quite a lot, as it happens.

As part of his search for deeper meaning, Stephen Moles decided to disconnect from his fellow humans after their habit of reducing complex ideas to 140 characters became widespread, and he attempted to discover what the *original twitterers* had to say instead.

Arming himself with a notebook, a pen and a strategy for translating their tweets into English, he went to interview the birds in their homes. He did this by walking around woodland areas while reciting the alphabet over and over again in his head and jotting down the letter he was on whenever he heard a bird try to convey something with its voice.

The end result was a vast archive of bird words (or "bwords") which is currently housed in the Dark Meaning Research Institute's secret underground liboratory. It contains entries such as "gwillterposch", "bemsbunsh", "hesperryheha", "oytiwincks", "fotizosh", "whoulamang" and "ghilowrax".

These are just some of the words that Stephen Moles found to be trending on the avian social network. **#kwank** was another, and it seemed very meaningful to the writer, so he made use of it in his work as part of a heartening message to those who had unknowingly brought him into existence:

There is a way out, via the Globe, the Swan, the Rose, the Hope, to a place where all the suffering finally has a purpose— the birdman who was the eggman is already flying out of something that hasn't even been described yet. It is a vision of beauty, ours to see in all its brightness, with other rare and undescribed animals, designs copied from nature and curiously coloured after life.

"THE green language", also called "the language of the birds" or "the language of unsaying", is a supposedly perfect means of communication. It is believed by some to be a universal language which was spoken by all creatures until division entered the world; others believe it is a form of secret communication that allows birds to communicate with the initiated.

"When for much my love that happy heart; world of paparazzi, my love green girl parasol."

'I am a thought in the mind of the forest,' said Stephen Moles. 'The birds singing are the neurons firing as the network of trees thinks me.'

*Grtash! Ploof! Kwank!*

When the words are read in the sequence they were given by the birds, they form a sentence that describes the path of energy through a higher mind when it thinks of the receiver of those words. This illustrates how, unlike regular language, this language of the birds works by uniting rather than separating: Shakespeare can be found in the character of Hamlet, and Hamlet can be found in the head of Shakespeare.

In order for you to have this thought right now, there may be somebody walking around your mind and building up a new language with the help of the environment, and that person may only exist because you are currently thinking them into existence.

How I wonder...**#wtf**

THE project grew from a tiny seed into a huge tree that stretched across the entire Globe. All kinds of travel became possible in the Bark of Millions of Years, but because it was structured like a Möbius trip thanks to a mystical space-time signature, the action led back to the centre. The two hemispheres of the big grey ampitheatre gave expression to night and day and the rotating hemicycle turned theatregoers into theatrecomers, up the Falcon Stairs and down the trapdoor within the evolutionary stage at one and the same time.

When all living things were spun out like vines and branches from the Cosmic Egg by the supreme deity of the Dogon people, the septenary structure of everything to come was inscribed on the bark of reality: 'Bird A loves Bird B forever and ever and over and over again.' The omphalus marks the navel of the world, where the two eagles sent out by Zeus came together, and the Globe is pulled by the force of grAmma into an ovoid shape that conceals the most wretched thing imaginable.

As I walked through the forest, I had the tune of the 'K-I-S-S-I-N-G' playground song in my head, but the lyrics were different somehow. Once I was finally able to see the words for the trees, a deeper meaning became visible in the spotlight of the glade. First and Last were sitting in a tree, forming a nest that housed the egg from which they hatched.

**Enigmama** @specialbranch 7yrs ago

Walking through the trees here reminds me of walking through a library. **#powderisland #books #magic**

The optical-fibre cables used in woods and forests are typically coated with a layer of bark so they blend in with the environment and are not noticed by most humans. Light signals are sent through the cables to express, in the vernacular of the stars, the beauty of a lightning strike or the poetry of a fatal car crash.

The flows in the cables can be interrupted and sections of scintillating text sliced off to make the pages of e-books. One of the best tools for editing a libretto is a mouth since it ensures a continuation of the flow of material through the body towards the anus with which it is connected. Beginning and end can both be wiped with sheet music made by the Dung Beatles, and the songs of the wires can be interpreted as portents that the murderer of Carmen will eventually be found innocent when it is revealed that the whole tragedy took place in the Theatre of Cruelty as a test of the unwitting actor's endurance skills.

The drama of Anti-Oedipus or Anti-Carmen Electra is laid like an egg at the end of the ordeal by an *Om* of the body's trap-door. First comes love, then comes marriage, then comes the most wretched substance in a baby carriage.

'ᚻERE,' said the professor, shining a light from his forehead as we came to a standstill in the middle of the forest. 'This is what you wanted to see.'

I peered through the bark which had become transparent due to the headlamp being shined onto it by the bword expert and I laid my eyes on a tiny feathered creature sitting in a nest of wires created by the entanglement of First and Last.

'It's a star-throated antwren,' he explained in a whisper. 'It's doing its bit for universal symbols. Some archetypes are endangered species, you know, and symbolic music acts need to be created to keep them alive.'

'Amazing,' I said. 'But why is it called star-throated?'

'Look...'

I poured my gaze down to where the spotlight from Ramon's forehead pointed and saw the nest begin to sparkle as light appeared in the wires.

> Bright are the stars that shine,
> Dark is the sky;
> I know this love of mine will never die,
> And I love her.

'Pretty Polly in the sky with diamonds!'

We had travelled such a long way, through the forests and the ruins of various evolutionary stages, and my endurance had been severely tested, but there was no doubt in my mind, as I watched the wondrous little creature describing reality in celestial symbols for us, that all the effort had been worth it. The growth of the tree had taken me to the centre of the seed; I was looking down at the drama on the stage of the theatre, but at the same time I was looking up, into the open air, at the players in the sky.

It was symbolism stripped of its symbols...*by its symbols, even.* It was like lifting the cover of *The Infinite Book* to view the unconscious of literature, like lifting the bonnet to see the archetypal engine running on a mysterious black liquid in the baby carriage.

'It's singing the light into existence and...'

'Yes, yes,' I interrupted. 'I know what you're about to say. I've seen the future.'

*Miroirs en obsidienne et en pyrite de fer, photographer unknown, ca. 2018. La langue en vert et la langue inverse, Theatre and Its Double, DMRI R24/64.*

$\mathcal{E}$ ARTH's mother tongue is the green language, the solumbrella that sprouts from the red breast of the earth. The shape of the branches of the trees in the forest are the letters of an ancient alphabet and each leaf displays lines which you can read between in order to get to the root of the problem.

By simply pointing this out and *leaving* more gaps than normal between the veins of these pages,

something

important

is

communicated

to

you.

*All's Well That Ends Well* is only complete when it's revealed to be unfinished...

A lost connection to the Tree of Meaning is re-established at the same time as a hole is punctured in the green parasol that was opened at the height of the Dog Days.

Still humming the 'K-I-S-S-I-N-G' song, I looked up at the night sky through the branches and made a breakthrough in my understudies. The tune rustled in the leaves is also written in the bark of the tree and the letters of the Hebrew alphabet are said to have been derived from the stars.

'I know what you're about to say...'

'I see what you mean...'

When the stars spoke about their reality they weren't

telling me about themselves; they were commenting on the blackness around them to give me the chance of finding my-self in the negative scenery. 'Speaking on behalf of all non-living things, white is a description of black, old chap, and the thing is to wonder what you *aren't*. The light and the meaning exist in the darkness of your ignorance, up above the world so high, like an egg laid in the sky by a Cosmic Goose.'

Plutarch called it

, the Leader;

but

,

,

,

,

, or simply

('the star')

[...]

AFTER spending the evening acting as a lookout for Sirius, I waited patiently in the heart of the forest beneath the paralune (the green parasol that was now being used at night) for Ramon to arrive and relieve me of my duties.

Just before the professor materialised among the mud and leaves, I thought I heard a group of insects rustling a popular tune but the name of it remained stuck on the tip of my tongue.

'Everything alright?' the professor asked as his headlamp suddenly shone into my eyes like an oncoming Lotus Elan.

'Oh, er...yes,' I said, feeling slightly startled. 'Sorry, I was miles away there.'

'Yeah, you looked it. I'd estimate you were as far away as Liverpool. Anyway, you've nothing major to report, right?'

'Right. Nothing to report. Apart from a bit of cryptographic sheet music, it's been a quiet night.'

'Glad to hear it,' said Ramon, slapping me on the back. 'Well, you're free to go. I'll take over now. Thanks for all your hard work.'

'No problem,' I said. 'Good luck and goodnight.'

'Goodnight, old chap.'

For some reason, I still felt like I was rooted to the spot even though I was free to go. As Ramon took up his position as the new lookout, I kept my watch for a few extra moments by staring at him while the lines on his face became deeper and the colour of his skin grew darker. Eventually the image of a human disappeared completely, and I was left looking at an ancient tree, strong and wise.

I wanted to remain at my post and interpret the lines of that mighty oak in the hope of gaining a full understanding of the septenary signature that had been carved into the bark of reality by bodies employed as artistic instruments, but for the time being the bark of the Dog Star seemed to be guarding against it, so I took my leave...

Back down Taymount Rise; left along London Road. A memory is just a thought travelling backwards in time. Right at the Esso garage, where the oil bubble would one day burst; up Honor Oak Road with the roots of the Tree of Life clenched in anticipation; a trail of sparkling breadcrumbs to represent the arrow of time. "That is my journey, and by journey I don't mean journey."

A memory that works backwards walks the backwoods so it becomes difficult to tell Hugin and Munin apart. The run-out groove following 'A Day in the Life' sounds like "Stephen Moles is a wanker" when played forwards but "he'll fuck you like a superman" in reverse, which is enough to make you wander through your green thoughts with a notebook and pen, creating inadverdant scryptures as you put your movements down in writing.

IN the Vedic scriptures, the story of two birds in a tree—one of them eating the tree's fruit while the other watches in silence—expresses something about the relationship between the lower and higher self. It is similar in some ways to the story of Adam and Eve, except the first story describes a rise while the Biblical one describes a fall.

When the lower bird stops eating the fruit and focuses on the higher one, it is finally able to move up to the same branch as its magnificent companion and realise that there was only ever one bird on the tree. Unlike regular language, this language of the birds works by uniting rather than separating.

The fruit eaten by Eve, on the other hand, creates the illusion of separation because the division of things, especially a person against their self, leads to a kind of knowledge, but of a very limited nature which needs to be transcended at some point.

Perhaps the Garden of Eden is Part One and the Tree of Jiva and Atman is Part Two of the same story, and the humans just turn into birds halfway through. Nommo, the first living being, split into four pairs of twins shortly after being created...

IT is generally believed that the Beatles were made up of four distinct elements (fiery John, watery Paul, airy George and earthy Ringo), but some people have posited the existence of an ethereal fifth member. Although the term "the fifth Beatle" is often used, there is no agreement about who this should be applied to, which means the total number of "fifth Beatles" is actually seven (manager Brian Epstein, producer George Martin, artist Yoko Ono, bassist Stuart Sutcliffe, drummer Pete Best, press officer Derek Taylor and road manager and personal assistant Neil Aspinall).

The recurring search for "the perfect fifth" therefore proceeds according to the same magical 7/4 time signature of 'All You Need Is Love' because the "Fab Five" consist of two separate parts, of seven and four.

Hidden inside the pentangular star is a cast of hidden characters and a great secret. They can be brought into the light by pointing out that the way to identify the ideal additional member of the symbolic music act is to sing the beginning of 'Twinkle, Twinkle, Little Star,' because the relationship between the first twinkle and the second twinkle expresses an ascending perfect fifth.

It should also be pointed out that the lyrics of 'Twinkle, Twinkle, Little Star' refer to Sirius the Dog Star, which is a binary star system consisting of Sirius A and Sirius B, or Twinkle One and Twinkle Two.

Yes, the place to which the newspaper taxis are tasked with taking the person listening to 'Lucy in the Sky with Diamonds' is the same place where the star in 'Twinkle, Twinkle, Little Star' is found: up above the world so high, like a dia*monde* in the sky. We follow the pentagram back to its origins and find it refers to Sirius, the star associated with the god Anubis.

Others have sought to build upon the four functions of the self by introducing an eightfold system consisting of the Fab

Four posited by Jung and an additional four "shadow" functions that nestle in the unconscious, far from the consideration of most people. Tucked away in a secret chamber within a secret chamber, down beneath the world so low, like a diamond in sha-dow, the group performs its duty as a Dark Hearts Club Band that backs up Sgt. Pepper's colourful players with a swirling vortex of biological sheet music that is only noted by the most perceptive audience members.

It should not come as a surprise to learn that whenever somebody looks up at the leading light in the sky above, an understudy in the form of a shadow of the stargazer is created below. Nommo splits into four pairs of twins as the new aeon dawns and om nom Nom-ar is Ra-mon in ba ka words, no?

LMOST all of the moons of Uranus, the seventh planet in our solar system, are named after Shakespeare characters. The five major moons are called Miranda, Ariel, Umbriel, Titania and Oberon, while the names of the inner moons include Cordelia, Ophelia, Puck, Cressida and Juliet.

Although Shakespeare himself was called the "Star of Poets" by Ben Jonson, there are no stars named after him, which has led some to call for this to be changed—if they knew about Will-Lam Shakespeare and his alien pens, however, they might change their minds.

The star is in the light instead of the light being in the star, and the largest amount of luminosity is reflected to Earth at the height of the Dog Days, when Sirius is closest to our planet and your gaze is a mirror that splits Sgt. Pepper in two to reveal, among other things, a bulbous-headed alien lurking in the foliage.

According to the Voyager 2 theatregoer, Uranus XI said:

> Come, gentle night, come, loving, black-brow'd night,
> Give me my Romeo; and, when he shall die,
> Take him and cut him out in little stars,
> And he will make the face of heaven so fine
> That all the world will be in love with night
> And pay no worship to the garish sun.

The tomb was a womb, and when everything was correctly aligned, a starseed was deposited inside it. You are moving about in your mother's womb, in the Queen's Chamber of the Great Pyramid, and you are about to come across evidence of initiates being crowned with feathers to symbolise the soul.

Bright are the stars that shine and dark are the hearts of the members of the silent backing band.

WHEN I was a child, I heard the following conversation between two birds in my neighbour's garden:

'I'm carrying a terrible secret around inside me,' said Bird A.

'Tell me about it,' replied Bird B. 'We all are.'

'No, but this is a *really* bad secret. It's far worse than most, and I don't think I can contain it anymore. My heart feels so dark and heavy.'

'But you've got to carry on, especially if it's as bad as you say it is. The early bird catches the worm and seals it up with all the other worms in a can that, like Pandora's box, can never be opened. If it weren't for us, human civilisation would collapse.'

'I know, I know,' said Bird A, shrugging its wings. 'But it's just so hard.'

'You need to keep your beak up and keep singing, old chap. There's no other way.'

'But fear is eating away at me.'

'Fear? Fear of what?'

'Well, I've been thinking...if a book contains a description of a book spontaneously combusting, and that book contains a description of a book spontaneously combusting, and that goes on *ad infinitum*, then it would be very, *very* surprising if the first book we perceive didn't set itself alight at some point. Do you get what I'm saying? What if the secret has a secret? That would mean the secret of the secret also has a secret, and then...then...oh *Mortimer His Fall*, we're fucked!'

'Calm down! This is how the process of kwank starts, but it doesn't have to be a bad thing. There *is* a way out of the Theatre of Cruelty, a genuine cause for optimism, a hope of revitalisation...and the best thing about it is that it's part of you.'

'Really? What is it?'

'It's called the Loving Feather of Everything,' Bird B announced tunefully. 'You just need to work out how to find it. Meet me back here beneath the Evening Star and I'll tell you more about it...'

'AND that is the view of Voyager 1.'

'I disagree. I think the two birds on the tree represent the two hemispheres of the brain. One side acts while the other observes, and this is how consciousness works. I'm not sure if I'm in a demisphere in the hemisphere in the supersphere or what, but I'm looking up at the dome of twinkling stars in the open-air Globe and it feels like a distinct possibility that I'm wondering myself into existence.'

> First and Last sitting in a tree, K-I-S-S-I-N-G,
> How I wonder what you'll be...
> And I love her.

'Also, I think Lucifer, the Morning Star, was good. The so-called Fall of Man is only a fall if we don't make good use of the knowledge given to us by the light bringer. The ascending fifth is the sound of the veil being torn down.'

*Which view is right?*

'I'm not sure if by "right", you mean "correct" or "dexter", but in either case the answer is that both are right: one is "left-correct" and the other is "right-correct". They are enantiomorphs of truth.'

> Just then flew down a monstrous crow,
> As black as a tar-barrel;
> Which frightened both the heroes so,
> They quite forgot their quarrel.

You can see in the reflection in the window of the kebab shop or on the surface of the mysterious black liquid that they are Part One and Part Two of the same thing, and that the humans assume the role of Volatees halfway through the play.

To have the illuminating thought that Nothing and Everything are twins, there needs to be a researcher, whom you have wondered into existence, strolling through the trees on the stage of your thoughts and leaving a sparkling energy trail of known secrets. His footsteps are electric breadcrumbs that map out the wonder you feel at not being able to separate yourself from the star of the show in the Globe Theatre.

'Yes, I'm leaving, but it's in order to destroy the illusion of the material world...then we can be reunited in the light of truth. You understand, don't you?'

'Yes, I understand. It's Shakespeare in Hamlet and Hamlet in Shakespeare, Paul in Ramon and Ramon in Paul, Sirius A and Sirius B, e-book and p-book. It's Hugin and Munin closer than you'd think and exactly as close as you think at the same time.'

The dome of the sky was likened to a skull in the Gothic Mysteries and the birds flying inside it were the thoughts of the deity. The names of Odin's two avian messengers, Hugin and Munin, meant "thought" and "memory".

> When I get younger growing my hair
> Many years ago,
> Are you still deliv'ring me a valentine,
> Wormhole greetings, needle of pine?
> When I stay out in the shade of a tree
> Do you sycamore?
> Do you still need me,
> Do you still feed me,
> When I'm twenty-four?
> Every summer we can rent a kennel on the
> Isle of Dogs, if it's not too hot;
> We shall at-om bomb.
> Ancestors on your knee:
> Harry, Dick, and Tom(b).

THE Egyptian idea of the *ba* represents the unique essence of an individual. It is depicted as a bird with a human head and can be seen flying out of the tomb described in this sentence to unite with the spiritual double, called the *ka*.

The *ba* can also be seen sitting in a tree close to the tomb in the previous paragraph. It might fly off somewhere but it won't go far, and it will always return to the body each evening.

Just as I finished the description, a bird with a message attached to its leg suddenly flew in through an open window and began pecking at the bread I had baked earlier that day. Although the appearance of the animal was completely unexpected, the thing that surprised me most was my calm acceptance of it. The creature's message of peace and love seemed to instantly rub off on me, and I felt able to enjoy the novelty of the situation, the first rays of the coming summer of love following all my nocturnal activities.

While Jung was attempting to treat a female patient who was "psychologically inaccessible", a beetle flew in through the window immediately after the young woman recounted a dream about being given a piece of jewellery in the form of a golden scarab beetle. The psychoanalyst caught the insect in his hand and gave it to the woman with the words, "Here is your scarab", which "punctured the desired hole in her rationalism" so she could then be treated successfully.

I unfolded the message brought to me by the bird and smiled an irrational smile. *The mystery of death could be solved... Whatever survives the destruction of the mortal envelope can progress to the higher branches...*

Perhaps there was no bird in the room at all, or perhaps I was the bird and the bird was me. *Somewhere in the night, I am writing a message to myself...*

Some said the water was poisoned and the air was dangerously thin where I was, and that the visions brought on by drinking and breathing could be fatal. I didn't disagree with them, but I had no faith in the implicit idea that the "unpoisoned" water of life and the voluminous breathing material produced by the trees were not normally meant to produce visions.

In 1964, when Beatlemania was at its height, the Scarab Beatles toured North America and played in 24 venues, one of which was the Red Rocks Ampitheatre in Denver. The Denver concert was the only one on their Unholy Land tour that did not sell out. While they were there, the group frequently complained of being out of breath and had to have several trees placed on the stage to provide additional oxygen.

The average tree produces around 100kg of oxygen in a year, and contains around 100 books. The gold-green colour of the insect messenger sent to Jung was close enough to that of the golden scarab in his patient's dream to be able to puncture a hole in the young woman's "geometrical idea of reality" and let some air in.

SOMETIMES time is timeless. Sometimes time is just a line of ink flowing like a river across the thin sheet of air along Honor Oak Road, then bending like a ray of light from the Dendera bulb around the diesel pumps of the Esso garage. Walking up Taymount Rise, a seemingly normal English gentleman can leave a trail of breadcrumbs through Forest Hill so the birdman can find his Way.

I knew that beginning the day by breaking the seal of the bread and stirring the black sun of the coffee was an extreme measure, but I felt that it had to be taken—the bread of one's life has to be consumed at some point, and my *ba* was getting peckish.

When I reached the circle of trees which was infinitely bigger inside than it appeared from outside, I threw the last few crumbs down and felt the green parasol begin to vibrate as the forest checked my identity. Electrical sparks connected up the seven ONE WAY signs for a timeless moment in a bright circle and the hidden world within was revealed to me via a sudden pineprick from death.

*I was free to enter.*

If a tree falls in a Calabi-Yau forest, most humans won't hear it, even if they are standing right where it happens. To dark meaning researchers, however, it sounds like the seven thunders, and it can point The Way to where the music of the self can be heard.

A voice told me to seal up in a complex manifold of flesh what the seven thunders had said and never put it down in writing.

'If every Tom, Dick and Harry can read the sheet music of the Dung Beatles, all hell will break loose.'

'Ommmmmmm...'

'Stick it where the sun don't shine!'

'yAUM!'

22

I disobeyed the voice and called my disobedience *The Most Wretched Thing Imaginable*.

I hope you enjoy reading it.

THERE are seven words that the censors forbid people from saying on radio and television because they are considered unimaginably filthy. They are: *shit*, *piss*, *fuck*, *cunt*, *cocksucker*, *motherfucker* and *tits*. This means that the work of William Shakespeare, which contains a mention of a "pissing-conduit", and the Bible, which refers to "he who pisseth against the wall", are both deemed inappropriate for public broadcast.

The seven symbolic seals on the book mentioned in 'Revelation' could only be opened by the Lamb who proved himself worthy of looking on the contents:

> And I saw when the Lamb opened one of the seals, and I heard, as it were the noise of thunder, one of the four beasts saying: 'Shit!'

> And when he had opened the second seal, I heard the second beast say: 'Piss!'

> And when he had opened the third seal, I heard the third beast say: 'Fuck!'

> And when he had opened the fourth seal, I heard the voice of the fourth beast say: 'Cunt!'

> And when he had opened the fifth seal, I saw under the altar the souls of them that were slain for the word of God, and for the testimony which they held. And they cried with a loud voice, saying: 'Cocksucker!'

> And I beheld when he had opened the sixth seal, and, lo, there was a great earthquake; and the sun became black as sackcloth of hair, and the moon became as blood;

> And the kings of the earth, and the great men, and the rich men, and the chief captains, and the

mighty men, and every bondman, and every free man, hid themselves in the dens and in the rocks of the mountains;

And said to the mountains and rocks: 'Mother-fucker!'

And when he had opened the seventh seal, there was silence in heaven about the space of half an hour.

And I saw the seven angels which stood before God; and to them were given seven trumpets.

And the seven angels which had the seven trumpets prepared themselves to sound.

And I heard a great voice out of the temple saying to the seven angels: 'Tits!'

Opening the seven seals and reaching into the body to spin out the starseed is a filthy job, but someone has to do it.

OVER the years, many people have wondered how the apocalyptic word "buckarastano" was discovered—but now that Stephen Moles has revealed his technique for transcribing bwords, it seems the mystery of its origin has finally been solved.

Walking through the woods and breathing the chitzum air with my business partner was a transformational experience, and I realised something important, like how Hugin and Munin or matter and antimatter are the same thing travelling in different directions through time.

'When did you get these buckarastanos made up?' I asked him. 'We've been together pretty much all day and night. There aren't any shops for miles —only trees.'

'You've just answered your question, old chap,' he said with a wry smile.

I thought I understood how it all started, but...

*ba ka ra sta*, no?

> "Someone will understand the importance of this and will continue the research if anything happens to me, but I urge anyone looking into the B*ckarastano to proceed with the utmost caution."

'Where did that quote come from?'

'From a book in the heart of the Ecolibrary. Take a look...'

TITLE: *A true & faithful relation of what passed for many yeers between Professor Donaldson and some spirits : tending (had it succeeded) to a general alteration of most states and kingdomes in the world*

Paperback, 488 pages

PUBLISHER: Hawker Perennial

LANGUAGE: Green

As soon as I stepped into the library I could hear the low hum of the stories of life and death moving around inside the wires like diesel trucks. An owl sitting on a lower branch was overseeing the journey of a tale about a traffic accident from one section to another to make sure it arrived safely at the moment of impact, while its colleague higher up in the same tree was supervising a murder-suicide as it made its way to the newspaper archive.

It was a beautiful night inside the book grove, with the leaves swaying gently in the breeze and the stars out in full swing, and I would have happily stayed there all night, but I had to leave as soon as I found what I was looking for because I had so much more to do.

After rummaging around inside a nest of books, I found it: *The True Story of Baucis and Philemon, a Sequel to The First Ever Human Being to be Saved by the Loving Feather of Everything, Containing Elements of Other Works Such As Oh Time Thy Pyramids, to which is added a Brief and General Idea of the Creep and Relaxation of Nonlinear Viscoelastic Material Inside the Philosopher's Egg.* It was a book that followed the traditional Shakespearean five-act structure but because it was also written as a repeating cycle of stressed and unstressed characters using the mystical 7/4 meter, the fifth act contained ever smaller additions to itself like trapdoors within trapdoors that led to the very centre of the action. The falling pentamatter of the trees was of an ascending fifth Beatle that led the way to the green girl with the sun in her eyes, up above the world so high.

I looked up and saw the stars dropping huge hints about their reality—'Sta is *star* in Tok Pisin, no?'—so it seemed like a good time to leave: I was ready to hatch out of the darkness like whatever was inside the *eBook of the Dead* and see what the light had to offer.

'I plan to smuggle this egg through customs when I make my final journey,' I announced to Ramon as I displayed my prize to him on the outskirts of the forest.

'You realise how dangerous that is, don't you?' the concerned professor replied, motioning with his hands for me to put the egg back under my coat. 'If the dog-headed customs officer gets one sniff of that...'

'I know, I know. It'll be the end of me. But it's the end of me whatever happens when I'm taking my final trip, isn't it?'

'Yes, I suppose you're right. One way or another it's the end of you.'

'But the beginning of my honeymoon period,' I added as I put the rare object away. '*Hopefully...*'

> Bright are the stars that shine,
> Dark is the sky;
> I know this love of mine will never die,
> And I write to her a love-line.

—*All's Well That Ends Well*, Act II, Scene I.

'You citeseeing already?' Ramon said with a warm smile.

'Yes,' I replied, my eyes fixed on the stars. 'I'm planning to leave, so why not? I want to explore everything under the sun and you're going to help me. In the next life, you're going to reprise the role of the wise professor and invite me on your trips around the world, and that's how I get to take the *final* trip. It's going to be tough and I'll have all kinds of horrors to endure, but hopefully I'll remember that they're just illusions to test me. If I can survive "life", I'll hatch out of its darkness and be born properly, as a Siamese twin of my love.'

'I see!'

'YES, I'm leaving,' said the male Liver Bird. 'But it's in order to destroy the illusion of the material world...then we can be reunited in the light of truth. You understand, don't you?'

'Yes, I understand,' the female Liver Bird replied. 'You don't need to say anything, my love. It's all in the scrypt.'

The two birds perched on top of the Liver Building in Liverpool are said to be a female and a male, the former looking out to sea to make sure the seamen return home safely and the latter looking towards the city to see if the pubs are open. It was often said that if the birds were ever to fly away, the city would cease to exist.

The birdman might fly off somewhere but it won't go far from the corpse of the city or the wreckage of reality. When night comes again, a pair of darknesses will be cryptogamously created to complement the male and female twinkles that burn with love for one another at opposites ends of the tomb.

When the egg comes out of the body, the orifice says *Om*, the word that represents the beginning and end of everything. Sometimes the anus doesn't know whether to be an anus or a mouth, as Deleuze and Guattari point out in *Anti-Oedipus*.

'Eggs, eggs, eggs...All you need is eggs to start the day. Oh, and bread, coffee, biscuits and newspapers are also welcome. You may even find bacon, liver and salmon useful too.'

Many people eat eggs for breakfast, but when it comes to a Cosmic Egg, it takes a huge amount of courage and perseverance to smuggle it through the long, dark night and get it on a plate for when the sun rises. According to the Dogon people, famous for their advanced astronomical knowledge, the universe originated from a World Egg which was brought into existence and then cracked open by Amma, the supreme deity, who spun out the yarns of all living things from it and created Nommo, the first living being who later split into pairs of twins.

The Dogon were aware of the existence of the twin of the star Sirius long before it was detected by western astronomers with telescopes. Many people have asked how they acquired this knowledge, just as others have asked how Paul McCartney came to meet his alternate self and how Stephen Moles discovered the Buckarastano.

I am certain it will mean both nothing and everything to you if I say that the contents of the egg must be kept secret in order for it to hatch properly when the time is right. The dolphins lay their eggs in the tomb and the Nommo egg is *om nom nom nom*, dear Watson.

APTISM is the religious practice of immersing a biscuit in a pool of coffee in a baptismal cup or mug. Just as Jesus died, was buried and rose from the dead, so the biscuit goes down into the darkness of the coffee and rises again with a new and improved flavour.

People who are not worthy of the food will be destroyed by it. Those who are already sick will experience it as a sewage-soaked funeral biscuit and be forced to eject it due to a bout of violent vomiting and diarrhoea, but the Lamb will enjoy a fresh Sunshine biscuit that rises in the east and drops its crumbs across the globe while travelling further and further away from its home, to others that we humans know not of.

Having just finished my liver and eggs, I was sitting in my study playing the part of John the Dunker with a sacramental Viennese Whirl in the holy waters of my morning drink when a bird with green-gold wings suddenly flew in through the window.

I thought the bird would want to leave at the first available opportunity due to being in an unfamiliar place but something was keeping it there—the smell of the coffee, the sparkling energy trail, the philosophy of the plays of Shakespeare unfolding in your hands like magnum opus petals to reveal the most wretched thing in the world. When I pointed at the open window to indicate that it was free to go, the creature just hopped onto my hand like an acausal connecting principle.

After a couple of minutes, I put the tiny messenger down on my desk so I could begin writing a letter. From a bird's-eye point of view, the trail of black ink I created on the paper with my pen looked like a chaotic river turning self-aware circles in a landscape of pure white thought. Although my feathered visitor could overfly all the twists in the plot, including the attempt by a giant serpent to attack the pen, it seemed happy for the time being to simply peck at the remains of the body of Christ, the Lamb of God in bread, while waiting for the edges of the paper to come together and create the final destination.

> *Dear Professor,*
>
> *Thank you so much for your kind offer. I would love to fly out to the new world and study the Birdon race. February 23 would be an excellent time to start. And it would be a huge honour for me to be able to continue your invaluable research into the mysterious B—*

I looked up to see the messenger fly back out of the window. Although I hadn't finished writing my letter, the sight of the bird taking so purposefully to the air confirmed that my message had already reached its spacetime destination because here and now were there and then.

'I've seen the future.'

I looked up at the sky again and saw that the feathered creature was now a giant metallic bird carrying me like a human letter to my destination overseas.

I saw my higher self look out of the window of the silver bird. I was a ripple of ink, a twist in the river of the story that I was scrutinising from an editorial position. I waved to myself and slipped away, leaving only a watermark of the Fall of Man.

'All of human history has taken place on that tiny dot,' the captain of the plane announced as the other passengers began unwrapping their biscuits and sipping their coffees. 'Beauty is ours to see in all its brightness. It really puts things into perspective, doesn't it?'

*aradisaea rudolphi*, the scientific name of the blue bird-of-paradise, commemorates the Crown Prince Rudolf of Austria, who died in a suicide pact with his 17-year-old mistress, Baroness Mary Vetsera, in 1889. Rudolf shot his lover in the head and then shot himself.

Prince Rudolf's father, Emperor Franz Josef I of Austria, had no other children, so his brother, Karl Ludwig, was next in line to the throne. Archduke Karl Ludwig, the father of Archduke Franz Ferdinand of Austria, died in 1896 due to an infection picked up by drinking water from the River Jordan while on a pilgrimage to the Holy Land.

Today, pilgrims are frequently warned not to bathe in the river where John the Baptist is said to have baptised Jesus, as it is full of raw sewage. People bathing in such waters run the risk of catching a wide range of illnesses, including an E. coli infection.

Researchers have found a way of using the genome of the E. coli bacterium as a device for storing complex information. This opens up the possibility of saving image and text files in living cells.

*Perhaps my life story is a text in an E. colibrary within the body of a higher being. Perhaps Karl Ludwig was killed by swallowing someone else's life story.*

These genomic tape recorders are also called SCRIBES (Synthetic Cellular Recorders Integrating Biological Events). Thoth, the ibis-headed Egyptian god of writing, was also a genomic tape recorder, and he was tasked with recording the verdict on the deceased in the Hall of Ma'at and maintaining a great library of scrolls.

*Perhaps the tablets of light on which my actions are written are the bricks from which the library is built, and the words form a language of the birds that unites rather than divides.*

Thoth was also referred to as Lord of the Divine Body and the Voice of Ra. Along with Ma'at the winged goddess of truth, he accompanied Ra the hawk-headed solar god on his voyage on a sun barque, all the while keeping an eye out for deadly snakes in the waters. *I knew it was a drastic measure, but I felt that it had to be taken.*

In the underworld, the hearts of the deceased were weighed against the feather of Ma'at. Only those whose hearts remained balanced against the principles of truth and justice due to having led a virtuous life were permitted to proceed to Aaru, the Fields of Reeds, where souls existed in eternal bliss.

'How about we make a suicide pact?' Bird A said. 'We're both carrying terrible secrets around in our hearts; it's the only way to free ourselves.'

'No, no, no!' Bird B squawked. 'We're not in the Vienna Woods. Don't you remember what I said to you earlier?'

'Oh yeah. The Loving Feather of Everything. What is it?'

'The Loving Feather of Everything is the most beautiful and valuable thing in the world,' the second bird explained. 'And it's part of you. You can gaze upon it and see wonderful things that make all the suffering seem worthwhile. It's like a pine needle in a new life that branches out to a star with a trail of all possible secrets, a blessed vision of the body as an instrument that writes its unique spacetime signature in a mysterious substance like liquid vinyl on the title page of *The Book of Thoth*.'

'If it's part of me, where the hell is it? I've only got regular feathers on me.'

'It's hidden in a mysterious place somewhere deep inside you. It's sitting there patiently, clutching its unearthly signs of orientation, the master plan for all personal myths, while waiting to be spun out by the lowly little understudy who recognises himself as the guide of the Birdon people. You have to find a way of unlocking it, so the cell cracks open and the Loving Feather of Everything bursts out. It's the magical and ritualistic kernel hidden in the shade of the final act, the most beautiful secret in the world.'

'I've had enough of secrets!' Bird A complained, throwing up its wings in despair. 'I want to be free of them.'

'But you will be free if you can find a way to make this feather grow. If you're being weighed down by the dark secrets of human beings, then you need to see them as a trail of breadcrumbs that can lead you to your freedom. The way out of the dark woods is the Way In in reverse. There's a lot humans don't understand about feathers, right?'

'Right. So should we tell them?'

'No, you tit! That's the last thing we should do. We should quietly watch over that confidential information on behalf of the chick with the sun in her eyes.'

'I see.'

'Let's take the tufts on the head of the great horned owl...humans don't know what they're for, so you combine that mystery with the secret of, say, an undercover human spy murdering a young woman simply for being in the wrong place at the wrong time and witnessing a misdeed, and you're up and away, see? 100kg of oxygen, 100 wingbeats per second, 3,000 selves, 10,000 years, 20,000 starlings...The burden is felt by the self, but its heaviness is incredibly valuable if you use it as a ballast. The tufts are now just the tops of the trees, now just features on the map...You see what I'm hinting at?'

'I've got an inkling.'

'Feathers are like leaves, trees, talking pages of an infinite book...human history looks like a pile of soggy newspapers from up here, doesn't it? It really puts things into perspective. And what do you think goes on in a Calabi-Yau forest when no one's there to witness it? That place they call the United Kingdom can be bounded in an eggshell and reborn endlessly as the undiscovered country in the direction of "in", further and further from your night terrors and your morning sickness, as Papua New Guinea goes on forever in a single pixel on the blue bird-of-paradise's plumage. Get it?'

'Fuck yeah, I get it!'

The male blue bird-of-paradise hangs upside down and shakes its blue feathers to impress females. Every hunter and forager, every king and peasant, every young couple in love are on display in a psychedelic vision.

Arriving by port, you make your way to the Cavern Club via Paradise St...

FTER Papua New Guinea, I visited the Holy Land. I wanted to test the hypothesis that the real fall from Paradise was the adoption of language because language quite literally marked the point where we fell from the Real. I suspected I might face the same kind of hostility that Professor Donaldson and others encountered for putting their opposition to words into words, but I was prepared for it.

When Eve bit into the Apple of Knowledge, the computer worm inside the forbidden fruit was transferred to her mouth, where it became the self-replicating Word. This meant that human beings could communicate "The Truth" of the universe by simulating it with language, but it came at a price: entrapment within the simulation. The holes left in the Apple of Knowledge by the computer worm are wormholes or secret booktunnels that lead out of the literareproduction and back to the Adamic language used before Man's descent into the world of representations.

Remember that the red earth was scooped up into Adam by Yahweh to smother a fire but that fire lives on in the earth, and in the water. Remember also that all the holy rivers of the world are polluted by humans because humans are the pollution they are trying to wash away in the rivers.

I visited the Holy Land to test the hypothesis that the way to regain Paradise is to read between the muddy brown lines of biological sheet music and see the voice as a sexual organ that lays an egg in Adam's throat for the future glory of the Hum-on people.

There is more than one John in the Bible, and more than one John in the Beatles. Baptist and Evangelist; Lenn-on and Lenn-off. There is also Jahbul-on, Ram-on, Professor Donalds-on, Dr Wats-on, Marjorie Camer-on, Ober-on, Ben Jons-on, Francis Bac-on, Bost-on, Lond-on, Salm-on, the Dog-on and so on and so off...

'Tell us of the God On, which is, and never knew beginning, and we will let you Out/In.'

'I already have.'

I N order to be allowed to their rooms, all travellers must answer three riddles posed by the Sphinx, who guards the hotel door in much the same way Anubis guards the airport security gate.

'Which creature hath four parts to its body in the morning, two in the afternoon; and three in the evening?' asks the Sphinx.

'Easy... the Beatle. Next?'

'There are two twins: one gives birth to the other and he, in turn, gives birth to the first. Who are the twins?'

'Paul and Ramon. Piece of piss. You'll have to try harder with the third one if you're going to catch me out.'

'Why is a raven like a writing desk?'

'Ommmmmmmmmm...'

Tomorrow, and tomorrow, and tomorrow...they all came at once and I found myself in the hotel dining room staring out of the window at the peculiar umbrella on the terrace which looked like it was made from human skin.

Suddenly, a strange figure with a bulbous head came and sat at my table, putting down a plate of food opposite mine. He introduced himself as The Way, even though he didn't say anything, and I knew exactly what was coming up.

I had no choice but to take part in a strategic breakfast battle...

My response to The Way's opening gambit was to go for the full English opening, which made it very clear to my opponent that I didn't intend to submit to his culinary offensive without putting up a proper fight. As soon as my breakfast arrived, The Way advanced a tomato and opened up the lines for his hash browns to move forward, but I blocked this with a fried mushroom. We then battled it out for control of the centre, which resulted in The Way and I losing two tomatoes and two mushrooms respectively.

Since his tomatoes were much bigger than the pieces I had lost, I felt I'd already gained the upper hand, so I tried to capitalise on this by bringing a black pudding into play and directly threatening his toast; however, a couple of moves later, it became glaringly obvious that I had left my bacon exposed by fighting a battle on two fronts, and I watched in horror as The Way moved in to claim one rasher and intimidate another. Although I was able to block him with a sausage, this gave him the opportunity not only to move his toast out of danger but also to send it across the plate and put me under further pressure elsewhere.

To most people, it would have looked like two men were simply sitting quietly, staring intensely at their plates and occasionally moving pieces of food around, but to the most perceptive audience members, it would have been apparent that a ferocious battle of silent words of power was taking place. Om, aum, yau, yaum, yum-yum, om nom nom nom, etc., a tale told by nobody, sans sound, sans fury, signifying everything.

Several moves later, as my most precious piece, the egg, was being chased around the plate by a piece of salmon and two hash browns, the end was very much in sight. In a mystical vision, I could see Augustus Egg crashing and burning as the ship's cook in a production of *The Frozen Deep* attended by Queen Victoria, the old image of the self brutally sacrificed in the secret chamber. Without having managed to put The Way's egg under the slightest bit of pressure, I threw in the napkin and conceded that I would have to meet the King of the Dead, who sits atop the metallic flotsam on the surface of a sea of jet fuel.

While staring through the window at the umbrella that was now becoming sunburnt, I swallowed my most precious piece like a snake, praying that the sun of all my wasted tomorrows

40

would make it safely through the underworld and pop out of my back door as *The Boston Globe*'s future newspaper taxi today, hot off the press, cold on the shore.

When I turned back and reached for my coffee to wash down the egg, both my drink and my breakfast opponent were nowhere to be seen. The enigmatic little man with a head like a bulb had given off golden silence as the most dramatic spectacle possible, vanishing into Deep Blue as the salmon turned 45 degrees in heat on the emerald table.

WHEN I was out on a tour of the local area in the blistering heat, I was told by my terrestrial guide that the pelican we saw symbolised Jesus Christ. When the bird feeds its young with its own blood, it represents the sacrifice that Jesus made to his disciples, my escort explained.

I managed to keep my beak shut, but I was very tempted to tell him that saying one thing symbolised the other was like saying the left hand existed to symbolise the right hand when in fact they can be used together to applaud something on a much higher stage.

My wordless overguide kept me on the straight and narrow, so I was able to maintain a dignified silence, ensuring the raven was like the writing desk because of an additional element which remained unseen by most people—smaller than the Beatles, bigger than Jesus, and almost identical to a mote of dust spinning round and round on the disc of black vinyl. When the Great Bird shook its tail feathers in the heavens later that evening, the name of the nightingirl was written in the sky with fireworks.

The ancient Egyptians believed that if the ibis, which was sacred to Thoth, were ever to be taken to a foreign country, it would die of grief.

All of a sudden I felt an affinity with that bird.

*Did I pass the door of the tomb and enter the hotel or did I pass between the statues with open and closed mouths and enter the afterlife? The air was thin and the stars were in full swing—I remember that much.*

Subsequent tours became a blur of Orphean and olive-tree warblers in the ruins of the ancient ampitheatre. Red rocks and liver down the whirlpaul. Ornithology, archaeology, waterfall and wave...

Will I ever get home? Did I ever leave?

INCE flying in from Egypt and dropping back into the English tomb beneath the stars like an old, dry leaf, I could hear the rustling of the most mysterious sheet music all over the surface of the forest. Then, one night, while standing in the Sirius spotlight that shone through the hole in the nightshade, it occurred to me that the tunes were those of the Scarab Beatles.

Although they were only performed by an insect tribute act, the songs were close enough to the original gold-green oldies in the girl's dream to be able to convey the important message that I would one day have to travel west, further west than I had previously dared, to the land where the air was paper thin and the water was poisonous black ink, and enter the deepest Cavern ever built by man so my endurance could be tested in the Theatre of Cruelty.

In ancient Egypt, the term "westing" was used instead of "dying", which reflected the journey of the sun into the black night that seemed to be death but was in fact the substance from which the following morning's coffee was made.

'I'm only sleeping.'

'I am the eggman, they are the eggmen...'

'All you need is death...'

As I waited by the green paralune for Ramon to arrive, I found myself applauding the movement of a vinyl disc up the charts with Jesus and a pelican until they irrigated the soil below with droplets of blood. *The egg must be crashed and the image of the self sacrificed if the me-bryo is to be glimpsed in the wreckage.*

'Enjoying yourself?' my colleague chuckled as he appeared before me suddenly.

'Oh, er...It's difficult to say.'

'It's OK. I understand. You don't need to say anything.'

'You've seen the...?'

'Yes.'

43

We both switched on our Lotus headlamps and stared at the wires of the forest until it was no longer clear whether we were illuminating them or they were illuminating us. After a few minutes, every branch of knowledge, both human and divine, had come to life and was twinkling a trail of secrets so we could finally see what the wood and the trees had been synergetically hinting at.

'The Ecolibrary!'

*The Man in the Moone...*

*The Singularity of the Baconian Cipher...*

*Cryptomenytices et Cryptographiae Libri IX...*

*Creep and Relaxation of Nonlinear Viscoelastic Materials...*

*Liquid Ring Vacuum Pumps, Compressors and Systems: Conventional and Hermetic Design...*

*Music Explained as Science and as Art and Considered in its Analog Relationship with Religious Mysteries, Ancient Mythology and the History of the Earth...*

*A Natural History of Uncommon Birds: And of Some Other Rare and Undescribed Animals, Quadrupeds, Fishes, Reptiles, Insects, &c., Exhibited in Two Hundred and Ten Copper-plates, from Designs Copied Immediately from Nature, and Curiously Coloured After Life, with a Full and Accurate Description of Each Figure, to which is Added A Brief and General Idea of Drawing and Painting in Water-colours; with Instructions for Etching on Copper with Aqua Fortis; Likewise Some Thoughts on the Passage of Birds; and Additions to Many Subjects Described in this Work...*

Suddenly I saw my life story pass through the vine, which transformed me into a wise old owl overseeing the journey of a tale about an air disaster to make sure it arrived safely at the moment of impact. Although it only lasted a moment, it was one of the most humbling experiences imaginable to see

44

my life spin out of control from the central seed and then, in praise of the force of grAmma, coil up into a foetal plane crash in which a new self was glimpsed.

I saw the news today, oh boy. It had a septenary structure and was inscribed on the bark of reality.

Each tree holds around 100 p-books...but e-books? Well, that's another story, or should I say, that's another several thousand stories. The mouth doesn't know whether it's slicing through reading material or breathing material, but if it has the will to keep going, standing firm with its roots in the ground while travelling faster and faster at right angles from 4D reality, it can absorb more and more brightly lit plotlines until trillions of scenes are taken in with every breath. In the unexplored direction commonly called "in", which is the spacetime equivalent of the perfect fifth, it can travel to infinity and become the root note of its own body which is reproduced as the Siamese twinkle above.

'I knew my years of watching would prove to be fruitful, but this...this is something else,' I said breathlessly to Ramon. 'I'm such a lucky man.'

'It's no less than you deserve, old chap.'

Before he turned to wood, the professor stared at the sparkling pixels of moisture on my cheeks and read a message reflected in them by the stars.

'Beauty it was ours to see in all its brightness when, amidst that happy company, world of paparazzi, we beheld with our eyes that blessed vision, our love green girl parasol.'

'What?'

'Your sweetheart,' Ramon said. 'The one you had to say goodbye to in your youth...'

'Polly?

'Yes. She says she's thinking about you...thinks about you every day, even after all these years of being blown around the

Globe. She says she hopes you're happy, and...'

*The First Ever Human Being to be Saved by the Loving Feather of Everything...*

'...she says look up...'

S HERLOCK Holmes looked at the *News from the New World* and received the navigational aid he was looking for. A coded message hidden in the obituaries section was like the bright white light of a newspaper taxi that took him south of the river to explore new frontiers in astronomy and journalism. In the eyes of the detective, all knowledge had been put down in writing because he knew how to read between the lines and see everything as a code—an apparent dead end as a new beginning; a plane crash as a Big Bang; the body as a secret message to itself, enfolded within skinsheets of biorhythmic music.

'Psst!' The leaves, with their dark veins and coded pixels, seemed to whisper secrets about a new world of undiscovered beauty.

The multiple meanings of a word or term provide a good example of how an essence can be used to both reveal and re-veil: if we are told that "The Way" is the most important element of turning somewhere in search of guidance, a first interpretation of the term as meaning "The Direction" can make us miss the additional meaning that could be derived from interpreting it as "The Manner" of the turning. This is an illustration of both how the manner in which we turn somewhere for guidance is overlooked and what that manner consists of. If we know *how* to look for the message, we can look *anywhere* and be sure of finding it.

'While the twofold difference in this illustration is illuminating, it is important to remember, if Polly is to see me, that there are always seven different possible meanings for everything, seven different tones sung by every bword.'

'More meanings? How I wonder what they are...'

'Well, here's another clue for you all...Just as we sometimes look *up* and *out* to the heavens and sometimes *down* and *into* our bodies in search of guidance from God and DNA respectively, so too do God and DNA look *down* and *up* to us respectively.'

'Yeah?'

'Yeah.'

'Let's do it!'

'Here,' said the professor, illuminating the path with his head-Lam as we passed the seven ONE WAY signs and entered the circle of trees. 'This is what you wanted to see: your Romeo cut out in little stars in the honeymoon period. One way or six others, it's the end of you but the beginning of a bright love-line shining out from between the songlines of Stephen Moles' obituary.

Strange all this difference should be

'twixt Sirius A

and Sirius B.

2464 [hide] v t e

## MONTHS AND DAYS OF THE YEAR

### January

1 2 3 4 5 6 7 8 9 10 11 12 13 14 15 16 17 18 19 20 21 22 23 24 25 26 27 28 29 30 31

### February

1 2 3 4 5 6 7 8 9 10 11 12 13 14 15 16 17 18 19 20 21 22 23 24 25 26 27 28 29

### March

1 2 3 4 5 6 7 8 9 10 11 12 13 14 15 16 17 18 19 20 21 22 23 24 25 26 27 28 29 30 31

### April

1 2 3 4 5 6 7 8 9 10 11 12 13 14 15 16 17 18 19 20 21 22 23 24 25 26 27 28 29 30

### May

1 2 3 4 5 6 7 8 9 10 11 12 13 14 15 16 17 18 19 20 21 22 23 24 25 26 27 28 29 30 31

### June

1 2 3 4 5 6 7 8 9 10 11 12 13 14 15 16 17 18 19 20 21 22 23 24 25 26 27 28 29 30

### July

1 2 3 4 5 6 7 8 9 10 11 12 13 14 15 16 17 18 19 20 21 22 23 24 25 26 27 28 29 30 31

### August

1 2 3 4 5 6 7 8 9 10 11 12 13 14 15 16 17 18 19 20 21 22 23 24 25 26 27 28 29 30 31

### September

1 2 3 4 5 6 7 8 9 10 11 12 13 14 15 16 17 18 19 20 21 22 23 24 25 26 27 28 29 30

**October**

1 2 3 4 5 6 7 8 9 10 11 12 13 14 15 16 17 18 19 20 21 22 23 24 25 26 27 28 29 30 31

**November**

1 2 3 4 5 6 7 8 9 10 11 12 13 14 15 16 17 18 19 20 21 22 23 24 25 26 27 28 29 30

**December**

1 2 3 4 5 6 7 8 9 10 11 12 13 14 15 16 17 18 19 20 21 22 23 24 25 26 27 28 29 30 31

PEOPLE have spent years searching for *The Book of Thoth*, which is said to contain all of the secrets of the universe. Thoth, who has the title of "Author of Every Work on Every Branch of Knowledge, Both Human and Divine", put all wisdom down in writing, according to one text which described the body of work that contained it.

*In the Forest of Babel, having read the book, I just had to look at the 365 different recordings of 'A Day in the Life' in search of the 366ᵗʰ one they concealed.*

People have spent years travelling across the world in search of the manuscript which is said to contain a spell that allows the reader to understand the language spoken by all animals; but the treasure was always much closer to home...The Egyptians stored texts in the "Houses of Life", which were libraries within the temple complexes, and the Egyptian historian Manetho claimed the body is a temple, every cell of which contains 36,525 books.

*It seemed as if the leaves of the annual could talk, and if it weren't for my bad dreams about audiobooks narrated by evil spirits, I would have been capable of discovering the navel in the head, the nutshell of infinity.*

In one book about *The Book of Thoth*, Setne Khamwas, a man who tries to steal the magnum opus from the tomb of Prince Neferkaptah (who was driven to suicide by the gods for stealing the book himself) is tricked into killing his children and humiliating himself in front of the pharaoh, only to discover that the experience was an illusion created by Neferkaptah, which prompts Setne to return the book to the tomb in fear.

*Did I pass through the door of the hotel and enter the tomb?*

Most people interpret the story of Setne Khamwas as a message that the knowledge of the gods is not meant for humans, which is correct in a sense, but that doesn't mean that humans shouldn't try to obtain it—it means they have to transcend themselves and become superhuman in order to grasp it, like the Lamb becoming worthy of opening the seals. Paradoxically, the way to do this is to carry the secrets of the gods around in your heart, to hold forbidden words in an unread breast, so you are strengthened by their extreme effects and the fatal becomes the foetal. Yes, it may be that the e-reader simulator was more than just a bit of fun—a *Jocus Severus*, much like the enigmatic book of uncommon birds.

If you can expand your mind until your life story resembles just one of trillions of tiny texts in a bookterium or an Ecolibrary, then the secret of the secret will be yours, but who or what will *you* be? Just as the effects of an E. coli bacterium are good or bad depending on which part of the body the microorganism is in, so the effect that a profound secret has on you will depend on what *you* are.

*How I wonder...*

Many birds are forced to carry terrible secrets around inside them, but they manage somehow. Perhaps *Human Kwank* is Part One and *Avian Kwank* is Part Two of the same story, and the humans turn into birds halfway through—after all, the unique essence of an individual was seen flying out of the tomb in a previous chapter to unite with the *ka*.

People who are not worthy of the information will be destroyed by it. The greedy, after having failed to crack open the egg due to the hardness of their own egoshells, will swallow the secret whole but will soon be forced to eject it due to a bout of violent vomiting and diarrhoea.

'yAaaauuummmmmm!'

Likewise, hateful individuals who try to make the Loving Feather of Everything grow out of them will experience excruciating pain.

'Motherfucker!'

The ibis, which was venerated for devouring crocodile eggs and driving winged serpents out of Egypt, resembles a heart when its head and neck are tucked under its wing. This beautiful bird is a muscle which, when flexed in the right way, can burst out in visual applause for the 7/4 ticker band and unite with its partner in the Great Bird of the Liverpolynesian night sky.

When Hamlet thinks Shakespeare, he becomes Shakespeare thinking Hamlet, and when he realises there was only ever one bird on top of the Liver Building, the scenery used to depict all the celebrated cities, from London to Alexandria and from Liverpool to Thebes, suddenly vanishes down the hole in the middle of the stage, following a run-out groove of twinkling breadcrumbs similar to the one that allow birds to transmigrate to others that we know not of.

When the main character in Francis Godwin's *The Man in the Moone* is carried to the titular planet by birds, he discovers the inhabitants all speaking a language made up of "tunes and strange sounds". As he begins to learn the lunar language, he understands the many potential meanings the words possess due to their interpretation being dependent on tone.

Two musicians may openly discourse with one another on the subject of polysemy without fear of being understood: "That is my lunar journey, and by lunar journey I don't mean lunar journey."

**#wtf**

THE first night of the Mysteries was under a new moon, when the negative scenery was in place and all the hints and instructions for the candidate were at their brightest.

With the Pythagorean doctrine of metempsychosis suggesting that each soul has its own star from which it came and to which it will one day return, the mystery players must have gazed into the vacwomb and wondered a great many understudies into existence on the opening night.

*A map of the stars shows the route to the self—it's the sky above or a person push*, I thought *to myself* in a love-line of twinkling biscuit crumbs up the sky chart.

'Sacred or magical language is not to be understood as a succession of terms with definite meanings,' my tour guide explained. 'The excitation of certain nervous centres causes physiological effects which are evoked by the utterance of certain letters or words which make no sense in themselves.'

*Grtash!*

ETTERS, words and symbols are everywhere; there is no aspect of nature that doesn't offer them. The dark roots of the trees forming underground sentences with the roots of the ferns; the alphabet of the stones spelling out The Way; the syntax of the snakes following Apep's orders through the watery chaos.

'I am the night,' they said to me in unison, grinning zigzags.

Beneath the canopy of trees, snail and tortoise shells whisper Chinese symbols to the explorer, while up above, through the gaps in the leaves, Hebrew letters can be seen describing their origins. Because the bark forms one continuous but twisted surface like a Möbius strip, every movement leads back to the beginning, so when the seeker asks for illumination as to the correct path to follow, he receives various shades of noise from the forest on the similarities between snakes and fault lines, feathers and leaves, trees and brains. Green Hermes and the polysemous birdgirl are glimpsed in the endless abyssidian mirror...

Suddenly, the earth shook every hunter and forager, every king and peasant of its blue feathers and caused an immense tremor for everyone in the library. I tried to put up my umbrella as soon as I felt the rumble, but it was too late—the reading material came crashing down in heavy tomes, making my head smart. The way the word "egg" fell into the phrase "An egg a day keeps the doctor away" helped the force of grAmma and I to understand beneath a tree how a secret tunnel to the undiscovered country could be opened up in the heart of the forest.

As we experienced that flash of inspiration, a bolt of lightning lit up the Tree of Meaning like a neural network, making visible the connection between Father Christmas and the death and resurrection of the sun god. It was now the turn of the "other" side of the Möbius bark to tell the story of *All's Well That Ends Well, Including Me*, the gift of a book from a parallel universe...

'It's traditional in that place they call the United Kingdom to decorate homes with holly over the festive period,' it said. 'This practice is derived from the ancient belief that evil spirits are deterred from entering homes decorated thusly due to the prickliness of the leaves. As you can see, the leaves of this book have been made as smooth as possible in order to invite the supposedly evil spirits in and re-establish a lost connection to an ancient axis serving as the stage on which a curious family reunion takes place.'

Long-lost relatives meet in the placentre to observe the split between Dadd One and Dadd Two vanishing into thin air. The leaves vibrate like the ancestral instruments of birds in response to the sound of a disembodied, omniscient tour guide narrating the story of the beginning, middle and end all coming together, the leader of the Hum-on race always finally catching om to the indefinite meanings, the Sgt. Pepper seed being pumped along the veinyl songlines by the Lonely Heart and squeezed out of the monofold nervous centres of the body.

'Thoth was the Voice of Ra and he could seemingly hear my thoughts as I put them down on parallel pieces of paper in a secret act of disobedience,' I didn't say.

The sudden personality changes that many people undergo after travelling overseas are a form of escape from the horror of coming across a part of the divided self in a foreign country and recognising that the most important member of the Private Parts Club Band had lain helplessly in the mud ever since the om-phallus was axed at birth. 'I, ONE, I, X.'

A schizoanalysis of the basic substance on the artist's palette once the muddy colours of the Earth's shadow have been mixed in by Dadd, the son of Dadd, who is the figures of

Osiris, Set and Horus blended into one, reveals that the "normal" person is actually Part One of the same process of which the schizophrenic is Part Two. The end of the integration act occurs when the head is transformed into a centre of reality where darkness has no place to hide and the evil spirits are installed there so a scene of redemption can be enacted in the Theatre of Cruelty.

You can sail in any of the four directions on the compass, to any of the continents of the world, but you will always come back with an anthropological account describing members of indigenous oral tribes referring to written pages as "talking leaves" after seeing overseas visitors reading from books. The accounts of the "talking leaves" can themselves be "talking leaves" that come to life and whisper their secrets from the shores of the undiscovered country.

'Psst! Turn on, tune out and drop in, dead man.'

THE ancient art of celestial navigation allows an explorer to make their Way through the sea of dark secrets by following stars like a trail of twinkling breadcrumbs to others that we know not of.

Carl Jung, who identified the four fundamental ways in which the ego interprets reality (Thinking/Feeling/Sensation/Intuition, John/Paul/George/Ringo or North/South/East/West), was able to spin out his personal myth from the central seed in all four directions on the compass of the self thanks to this recognition.

Likewise, the painter Richard Dadd, who trained at William Dadson's Academy of Art and killed his dad, made use of the sights of the Orient in order to develop his myth in the years of confinement in Bethlem Hospital. His travels abroad and his association with Augustus Egg were regurgitated during breakfast and mixed together to create the sea of burnt umber on which he could set sail to meet himself in the middle.

Augustus Egg, who was a member of a group of artists called The Clique, which was founded by Dadd and others, painted *The Travelling Companions* shortly before his death in 1862. The oil painting depicts two almost identical young women facing each other like mirror images while travelling on a train. It is very possible that they represent two aspects of the same person and that the rhythm of the train is the same as that of 'All You Need Is Love.'

The ancient Polynesians made use of bright stars, particularly Sirius, as navigation aids when sailing across the Pacific Ocean. The "Great Bird" constellation consisted of Sirius as the body, and Canopus and Procyon as wingtips which divided the Polynesian night sky into two hemispheres.

'I'm watching to make sure the seamen return safely,' said

one of the great birds on top of the Liver Building. 'The stars are bright and the sea is dark.'

'Sorry. I was miles away there. What did you say?'

'I said:

Source Parallax, mas Distance, pc Distance, ly Distance, Pm Ref.

Henderson (1840) ~230 ~4.3 ~14.2 ~134.2

Woolley et al.(1970) 377±4 2.653±0.028 8.65±0.09 81.8±0.9

Gliese & Jahreiß (1991) 380.4±2.9 2.629±0.020 8.57+0.07-0.06 81.1±0.6

van Altena et al.(1995) 381.6±2.2 2.621±0.015 8.55±0.05 80.9±0.5

Perryman et al.(1997)(Hipparcos) 379.21±1.58 2.637±0.011 8.60±0.04 81.4±0.3

Perryman et al.(1997) (Tycho) (absents)

van Leeuwen (2007) 379.21±1.58 2.637±0.011 8.60±0.04 81.4±0.3

RECONS TOP100 (2012) 380.02±1.28 2.631±0.009 8.583±0.029 81.20±0.27.'

'I see.'

"DEAD reckoning" is a term that refers to the use of the self as a fixed point for the purposes of navigating when travelling by either air or sea. Arming himself with just a notebook and a pen, an explorer can follow directional cues communicated in the form of mysterious twinkles by what appears to be a distant spectator looking down on the action in the Globe Theatre but is in fact the secret star of the show. Instead of seeing the ego as the ultimate destination or the entire world, a researcher uses it as a way of understanding his true position in the universe and how far he is from the undiscovered country. He sets off from himself and is reborn as Christopher Colomphalus, the discoverer of the navel of the world, when he meets his higher self in the centre.

Having finally realised that he and the albatross were two aspects of the same thing, the mariner arrives home safely at the Pool of Life, where the Liver Birds have been waiting patiently for him.

'If we use the secrets of humans to navigate, what do humans use?' asked Bird A.

'God knows,' replied Bird B.

N 1927, Carl Jung had a dream about Liverpool in which he arrived by water and climbed up some cliffs, to where the air was thin, in order to see the "real city". In the centre of that city was a round pool, with a small island inside it, on which stood a single magnolia tree. The tree was in sunlight despite everything around it being "obscured by rain, fog, smoke and dimly lit darkness"; and at the same time, the tree seemed to be the source of the light.

The psychoanalyst described it as "a vision of unearthly beauty", adding that Liverpool was the "pool of life".

Although Jung never physically visited Liverpool, the location of his vision is said to be Mathew Street, where a venue made famous by the Beatles is also located. Arriving safely by port after avoiding the jaws of Apep, you make your way to the Cavern Club via Paradise St and test the hypothesis that the Faul from Eden was the adoption of language...

Apple Records was officially founded by the Beatles after their return from India in 1968. It was a sub-division of Apple Corps, which grew from a seed implanted in the body of Brian Epstein after he died. The interviewer seemed obsessed with all the recent trips the group had taken and asked them repeatedly about the meaning of their magical mystery tour. All the references seemed to point to a tomb or a secret bunker.

'Where is this bunker?'

'It's closer than you'd think.'

After Jung travelled to Liverpool in a dream, he says he experienced "a sense of finality" because he "could not go beyond the centre". Having realised that self is a principle and archetype of orientation and meaning, his personal myth began to grow from the central seed like a symbolic tree.

The Cavern Club was inspired by Le Caveau de la Huchette, a Parisian jazz club based in a subterranean building which dates back to the 16th century and is said to have been used by Rosicrucians and early Freemasons. The Quarrymen played there before being reborn as the Beatles.

In 1964, the insects produced music for the Beatlemaniacs by beating their wings together for around 30 minutes, which was more than enough time to communicate their heartening message of Rose and Hope to all those who had unknowingly brought them into being.

When the disc is rolled up the charts, the secret chamber of the heart is opened, and the music of the true self is heard. Boulder, Colorado attracted swarms of hippies in the 1960s for a reason—using their bodies as ancestral instruments, the so-called drop-outs sang the twinkles up above into existence. The light at the end of the tunnel was glimpsed through the branches of the trees when they looked up from their current evolutionary stage in the 1960s, the Red Rock Ampitheatre, a distinct possibility...

HE name for the Swan Theatre, built in London in 1595, was probably suggested to theatre builder Francis Langley by the multitude of swans that "beautified the Thames" at the time, according to Joseph Quincy Adams.

Playgoers arriving safely after navigating the dark waters of the Thames would step off the Bark of Millions of Years, fly up the Falcon Stairs and take in the message displayed by the Great Bird above the open-air tomb. The unspeakable was not unthinkable, and the Swan's capacity for cruelty meant the theatre could hold around 3,000 people.

After his visit to London in 1596, Johannes De Witt described the Swan as the "finest and biggest of the London amphitheatres", but it wouldn't be long before it became blackened and ruined, blurring the line between ornithology and archaeology, and art and death.

The Elizabethan authorities employed two informers, called Poley and Parrot, to spy on playwright Ben Jonson, whose play, *The Isle of Dogs*, caused a great deal of offence for reasons unknown to us after it was performed in the Swan in 1597. There followed a harsh crackdown on the theatre world by the Privy Council, which on July 28, the beginning of the Dog Days of summer, prohibited acting and ordered theatres to be "plucked down".

Although he would be later described by Jonson as "Our Star of Poets", William Shakespeare was, in 1592, infamously referred to as an "upstart crow, beautified with our feathers" by dramatist Robert Greene, who complained that the actor from Stratford-upon-Avon arrogantly believed he could write as well as the "University Wits".

Another University Wit, Thomas Nashe, also made a similar remark when he criticised writers who "in disguised array" vaunted "Ovid's and Plutarch's plumes as theyr owne". Nashe was the co-author of *The Isle of Dogs* play, on which some light is shed by a reference to Sirius the Dog Star in *Summers Last Will*, although that light is a most mysterious kind and it will mean both nothing and everything to anyone trying to look through the paralune for clues.

In the open-air theatre where the stars can be seen in the sky above as well as on the stage below, Hamlet makes a reference to the feathered hats which actors were famous for wearing at the time. He asks: "Would not this, sir, and a forest of feathers—if the rest of my fortunes turn Turk with me—with two Provincial roses on my razed shoes, get me a fellowship in a cry of players, sir?"

When Stephen Moles wrote his very own *The Isle of Dogs*, he was plucked to within an inch of his life by the 21st century Privy Council, but he carried on regardless, knowing that he was in possession of a secret feather that could not be touched by violence. *While waiting in the police cell, fingering a half-sovereign at the request of the custody officer, the enlightened murder victim is secretly flexing a muscle of opposition that can channel the rage of seven billion silenced poets and singers with one smash hit: shit, piss, fuck, cunt, cocksucker, motherfucker, tits!*

INTERROGATOR: Where are the files?

SUSPECT: What files?

INTERROGATOR: The files containing the intelligence you received from your contacts in the woods. Where have you hidden them?

SUSPECT: If you want information from the birds and the trees, just go and ask them for it yourself.

INTERROGATOR: We're asking you for it.

SUSPECT: Well, I haven't got it.

INTERROGATOR: We know you have because we've been

watching you. We put a Poley and a Parrot on your tail, and they observed you walking around the woods with a notebook and pen every single day between July 23 and August 23. What were you doing?

SUSPECT: Walking.

INTERROGATOR: Look...You realise you've committed a very serious crime, don't you?

SUSPECT: A Sirius crime?

INTERROGATOR: Yes.

SUSPECT: And what crime is that?

INTERROGATOR: Hacking.

SUSPECT: Hacking of what?

INTERROGATOR: Nature.

SUSPECT: Last time I checked, your job was to enforce artificial laws, not natural ones.

INTERROGATOR: I'm here to make sure society remains stable, and if I think someone's trying to undermine that, it's my job to stop them. We don't know exactly what it is you know, but we know you know too much for someone in your position, some-one who's nothing more than an upstart crow. Just hand over the information, stop your research, and we might go easy on you.

SUSPECT: There were other researchers before me and there will be other researchers after me...

INTERROGATOR: There were also other law enforcers before me and there will be other law enforcers after me. You'll just be another name in a long list of people who got their wings burnt after flying too high. Pythagoras, Dee, Donaldson, etc.

So just tell us!

SUSPECT: Ommmmmmmmmmm...

> Our Legates are but Men and often may
> Great State-Affairs unwillingly betray;
> Caught by some sisting Spies or tell-tale Wine
> Which dig up Secrets in the deepest Mine...
> Nor are King's Writings safe: To guard their Fame
> Like Scaevola they wish their Hand i'th Flame
> Ink turns to Blood; they oft participate
> By Wax and Quill sad Icarus his Fate.

—Bishop John Wilkins

In every instance where the power and influence of a forward-thinking and subversive individual reaches a "dangerous" level, the authorities will intervene. In many cases, the threat posed to the "balance" of society (that is, the *imbalance* of society which gives power to those at the top) is dealt with by absorbing it into the system via financial enticements, but when this cannot be done, the authorities will move things up to the next level with the use of personal attacks and disinformation in order to decrease the power of the message.

In the cases of Timothy Leary, Genesis P-Orridge and other countercultural figures, the Thought Police actually went as far as trying to *study and understand* the subversive messages they were opposed to. Vast collections of books and papers were seized by the authorities so they could be examined in detail, the idea being that whatever had the power to destabilise society could be found within the archive and then be either repurposed or indefinitely contained.

Stephen Moles placed the seed of the grand narrators' destruction in his archive so that the authorities would swallow it if they ever took action against him.

It is a buckarastano, it is a bomb.

Anyone who is not worthy of the secret will be destroyed by it.

*Grtash!*

RMING himself with a notebook, a pen and a revolutionary strategy, the researcher went to the woods to gather more information.

Just as the frequencies of different birds' songs develop according to which acoustic niches are available in the local environment, the nature of human beings' opinions is also dependent on which "opinion spaces" are available at the time.

If we hear someone voicing a strong opinion about something, we assume that the person is giving expression to something fundamental about their character—this assumption is correct, but the fundamental thing it reveals is the *purpose and function* of that person's beliefs rather than the beliefs themselves.

When, for example, a bird is in an urban environment with a great deal of low-frequency traffic noise, it will increase the pitch of its song in order to be heard better by other birds. If we were to analyse *why* the bird chose to express itself in that way, we wouldn't say it was because the one tone it chose over all the others was actually fundamental to its character and had to come out regardless of its environment; we would instead analyse whether the bird was trying to attract a mate, delineate territorial boundaries, etc., and then look at how its surroundings allowed that to happen.

Likewise, in the case of a person shrilly proclaiming, for example, that anyone who doesn't believe in the miracles of Jesus Christ should be put to death, we would look at the setting in which the statement was expressed and analyse whether the person was trying to attract or scare someone off with it. If the person was in a society where the vast majority of noise around them was of an atheistic nature, their opinion about Jesus would be very different to the same opinion in a society primarily made up of Christian fundamentalists. If we imagine someone in an atheistic environment choosing to occupy this "acoustic niche" of religious extremism because they want to differentiate themselves from everyone else, we can see how that person would have to voice an anti-religious opinion in a religious environment in order to express the same fundamental aspect of their character, which is the need to differentiate themselves.

The amount of time spent online by people squawking, crowing and hooting at each other, from the acoustic niches that offer the best expression of impulses that are so fundamental to their being that they remain ignorant of them, is shockingly huge. There are already more comment threads than books in the library, and the creepers are growing so quickly that humans are being strangled by the rants of people on the other side of the Globe.

'Mortimer, Mortimer, Mortimer...'

Nothing but 'Mortimer' to keep his anger still in motion.

When it is finally revealed to the public that half of the comments and opinions posted online are in fact an electronic form of birdlime generated by bots in order to trap the Hum-on people in niches and stop them flying above the forest to become Volatees, the speakers of a language that relies on subtle tones, it will be too late.

What can those creatures with their infamously tiny brains teach us?

**#missedflight #nightmare #stranded #wtf #sos #rumours #tomb #death**

CHRONICLER: In what language, good sir?

HERALD: Only by signs and gestures, for they [the lunar bird people] have no articulate voices there, but certain motions to music: all the discourse there is harmony.

FACTOR: A fine lunatic language!

'WORDS say little to the mind compared to space thundering with images and crammed with sounds,' declared Antonin Artaud as he set out his vision of a new kind of theatre in which words were used as blunt instruments against the audience. In *Theatre and Its Double*, he claimed that the text had had an oppressive influence on meaning and that 'a language of space, devoid of dialogue, which would appeal to all the senses,' was needed to liberate the magical and ritualistic elements from the red breast of the black earth. The leader of the Dark Hearts backing band steps out from the shadows and into the light to draw your attention to the dead body that was hidden in plain sight the whole time...

As the shittr of the West sank behind the trees and blushed in silent pigment, Artaud worked on a buckarastano of "impossible theatre". He hoped that the violence or cruelty of patricide, a murder-suicide or a fatal traffic accident would shock people into seeing beyond the false reality instead of fearfully returning the magnum opus to the tomb and begging the theatre gods to forgive them, but his vision was crushing. In order to make it a reality, he had to become the shittr himself and sink behind trees into the same dark mess of paints that Richard Dadd had to sift through in the mental institution, from bright pink to burnt umber the sun.

Like Dadd, Artaud, after a mind-altering trip abroad, was declared mentally unfit and was confined to an asylum which functioned as the prototype for the Theatre of Cruelty.

'I am my son, my father, my mother, and myself ...I don't believe in father, in mother, got no papamummy,' declared theatre-painter Antonin Artdaudd.

After reading the Egyptian *Book of the Dead*, seeing the geometric robes of Balinese actors as 'animated hieroglyphs' and remapping Mexico as a record of his journeys and bodily spasms, Artaud tried to extract a new language from the dark-brown mixture of space and sound. He realised that the only way to do this, the only way to leave the Theatre of Cruelty, was to squeeze through the anus of the mind and be reborn in a golden sound shaped like a zero. Smaller and smaller, through the parasol or arsehole, to be reborn in the dung egg as the God Om.

WHEN the sun shines in my eyes while I'm reading, the black ink appears red and the words seem to rise from the land of speaking blood. That green solumbrella, which waited so patiently in the black earth to be discovered by the reader's inquiring gaze, is brought to light at the height of the Dog Days and set up as both the parasol and the paralune in the centre of the earth's red bréost...

**Bréost**

Strong Feminine Noun

breast bosom stomach womb mind thought disposition richness fullness plenteousness plenty abundance copiousness fruitfulness fertility productiveness of mind character richness fullness of style or language copiousness fullness

Nominative (the/that séo) bréost (the/those þá) bréosta

Accusative (the/that þá) bréoste (the/those þá) bréosta

Genitive (the/that þære) bréoste (the/those þára) bréosta

Dative (the/that þære) bréoste (the/those þæm) bréostum

The "green language" or the "language of unsaying" was spoken by all creatures until division entered the world. The Globe was divided into Hemisphere A and Hemisphere B, the theatre and its double, and the understudy was forced to wait inside the central seed that would one day be spun out in all directions to spell out the 'BEATLES' in funeral flowers. To die, to sleep, to be resurrected along with all the non-local scenery, so the audience can, quite literally, *find themselves* among the ruins of the spectacle.

Artaud wanted to do away with the amphitheatre altogether and draw attention to the dead body that was hidden in plain sight the whole time. The cause of death was not documented, but it was rumoured that a pair of severed lips were found at the foot of a tree 20 years ago today.

I have seen a medicine
That's able to breathe life into a stone,
Quicken a rock, and make you dance canary
With spritely fire and motion, whose simple touch
Is powerful to araise King Pippen, nay,
To give great Charlemain a pen in 's hand
And write to her a love-line.

—*All's Well That Ends Well*, Act II, Scene I.

On the 100th anniversary of the deaths of Archduke Rudolf and his mistress, there were calls for the body of Mary Vetsera to be exhumed so the story about the manner of her death could be verified. The Hapsburg family had to intervene to prevent this from happening.

Rumours seemed to be growing over the corpse like bacteria. One historian said the tomb contained a total of 36,525 secrets. People were twittering about a murderous conspiracy to prevent Prince Rudolf's accession to the throne due to his support for Hungarian independence. Growth and decay had formed a pact of some sort...

In order for Rudolf to be given a Roman Catholic funeral and be allowed into the imperial vault in the crypt of the Church of the Capuchins in Vienna, a story had to be invented that the Prince did not kill his lover and only took his own life because he was temporarily deranged. The story was satisfactory enough to the Pope for Rudolf to be allowed to rest with the other Hapsburgs in the imperial vault.

'Give me problems, give me work, give me the most abstruse cryptogram or the most intricate analysis, and I am in my own proper atmosphere.'

It should be obvious by now, dear Watson, that what was in the grave depended on who was looking.

'Our love has given us feathers, so we'll fly through the door to the afterlife and enter a hotel at the end of time.'

'Yeah?'

'Yeah.'

'OK. Let's do it!'

The lovers found that simply looking into each other's eyes caused the feathers in the duvet to flutter. A moment of physical contact and the bed began to take off...

The newspapers said: 'Say, what you doing in bed?'

'She loves you, yeah, yeah, yeah...'

Two powerful wings sprout from the sides of the bed and lift you and the love of your life up into the air. Your body is no longer heavy, your woes are no longer yours. From your new editorial position, the landscape looks like a newspaper report on a tragedy and a scandal.

The blue bird-of-paradise hangs upside down in the sky, a star flies in through the window and drops its biggest hint yet...

INTERROGATOR: You've been flying all over the world on some sort of Magical Mystery Tour. We know you've been up to something. What is it?

SUSPECT: It is depicted as a bird with a human head and can be seen flying out of the tomb.

INTERROGATOR: Where is your secret bunker?

SUSPECT: It's closer than you'd think.

According to Socrates, a soul has to suffer being blown about for 10,000 years, in all directions on the compass and to all four corners of the Globe, before it can grow wings and return to its star nest.

ON numerous occasions, human beings have observed magpies holding "funerals". Many people have reported seeing the birds gather around the body of a "fallen comrade" before emitting loud noises, or words in a lunatic language, which are echoed by a huge number of other magpies in the surrounding area. The birds will also visit the deceased to lay grass or twigs over the body and hold a short, silent vigil before flying away.

When a human is choosing music for their funeral, they only consider human songs, but birdsong as a final send-off could be just the ticket for the birdman...

'A whole flock of family and friends convened around the deceased. One by one, they gathered things to lay over the body. One of them brought a pine needle and dropped it on him like the biggest hint yet.'

As the shittr of the West sank slowly into the dark portrait of Tara Browne behind the trees, the magical and ritualistic elements of the birds' behaviour emerged as an ovoid buckarastano of "impossible theatre". The actors gathered together and prayed for the dead author's soul to make it safely through the wires and to take up a new role as a pine needle in a new life.

'Who am I?'

'The twinkle in my eye.'

'I see what you mean.'

Literary field theory states that information cannot be destroyed, which means that death is not the end—it is simply a transition from nonfiction to fiction. As the form changes, it acquires new meaning.

When the Author dies, their soul enters the *Book of the Dead*, in which it is possible to become a lucid character if the 192 spelling tests are passed successfully. A truly lucid character is effectively their own author, guiding themselves safely through the undercurrents of the funerary text and into the literary afterlife. They establish the Rule of Three by becoming their own Holy Trinity of Author, Character and Reader. This closed circle is impossible to observe from outside but it can still be entered and experienced from within when birth and death become conjoined twins, one living and one dead, and a sense of closure becomes an opening.

'You're going to reprise the role of the dead Author and travel around the world in search of hidden meaning.'

*Ba ra ka sta, no?*

AGPIES are one of the few animals to be able to recognise themselves in a mirror. Since the ability to pass this test requires a sense of self and other, this may help to explain why magpies seem to mourn the passing of other magpies.

Hardly any animals are able to pass the self-recognition test, and the vast majority of gods also fail.

In ancient Mexico, obsidian mirrors were *seen* as portals to another world—and the word *seen* is the operative word here because it wasn't the mirrors that allowed people to see other worlds, but the act of seeing that allowed the mirrors to *be* portals. Tezcatlipoca, a central Aztec deity whose name means "smoking mirror", was often depicted with an obsidian seeing glass in place of his right foot.

As he was retracing the writer's steps through the ruins, the artist felt as if Tezcatlipoca was speaking to him and guiding his actions.

'I am the night.'

'I know. Now what?'

'Now you should place as many of those Rorschach ink mirrors around the world as possible so time and space become meaningless in themselves. People will be able to connect the blots and see backwards or forwards in time...and even into, through or out of space and time altogether. You should do it at the double. Got me?'

'Got you.'

Suddenly a monstrous crow, as black as a tar-barrel, flew in from D'en-vert, and smoking buckarastanos were found near the ruins of the temple, on the beach and in the jungle, at the foot of a tree. The silence was deafening.

Artaud's journey to Mexico was a voyage to "the land of speaking blood", where he hoped to make contact with the red earth which contained the pure white of the self that had been mixed in with all the other colours during the creative process. He stayed with the sun-worshipping Tarahumara Indians and, during an initiatory peyote performance, he managed to make the red rock of the ampitheatre roll away for a glimpse of light and a breath of air.

The colour of the Jung Beetle was close enough to that of his dreams for a hole to be punctured in the geometrical idea of reality.

In the various Mystery traditions, initiation takes place in underground caverns like those found beneath Denver Airport, where the lead character in the Theatre of Cruelty wanders around in darkness punctuated by flashes of light, and hears peals of thunder and the howling of dogs:

> SIRIUS ... SIRIUS ... SIRIUS ... SIRIUS ... Then a loudspeaker thunders, 'THE GOVERNMENT URGES YOU TO REMAIN CALM.'
>
> STUPENDOUS DISCOVERY. SKY PHYSICALLY ABOLISHED. EARTH ONLY A DOGGONE MINUTE AWAY FROM SIRIUS. NO MORE FIRMAMENT.
>
> These two forces, ours and theirs, had to be put in touch with each other.

INTERROGATOR: Now just hold on a minute, how the hell did you acquire knowledge of the Dog Star and its twin? Tell us about the God On.

SUSPECT: Why don't you ask the Dog-on?

*There is an answer to the question of why a raven is like a writing desk, but it cannot be put into words because a writing desk is like a raven.*

QUESTIONER: What is the work of this weekend?

MEDIUM: Geburah.

QUESTIONER: Geburah applied to what?

MEDIUM: The egg. The egg is resting on the point of mountain tops, very sharp. Water around, Lotus cars on it.

QUESTIONER: Egg is symbol of some new knowledge, isn't it?

MEDIUM: Gimel. Lamed.

QUESTIONER: What does that mean?

MEDIUM: I don't know; followed symbol of mountain and Lotus car.

QUESTIONER: How are we to break open the egg?

MEDIUM: In plain language it means: Thou art to go This Way. Out is In. On is Off.

QUESTIONER: That isn't plain language. How are we to get this new knowledge?

MEDIUM: Sow the seeds in the pyramid; go into the...into the Mother...to be born again.

QUESTIONER: What about the Mass of the Holy Ghost?

MEDIUM: That hasn't anything to do with it. You've shattered everything.

QUESTIONER: Tell us of the God!

MEDIUM: Om.

QUESTIONER: What the—?

MEDIUM: Ommmmmmmmmm...

QUESTIONER: Aaaaaaaaarrrrrgggggghhhhhhhh!

The reference to the Lotus car is a clue to help us understand how the egg can be broken open. One has to travel to the top of the mountain, where the gods reside, and enter the egg in silence through an identification with Lam; then, while seeing through the entity's eyes, one must descend in the mothership at high speed, following The Way Out to its inverted climax in the red nest of the earth.

*Grtash!*

Looking at the smouldering wreckage in the centre of the stage, it will be difficult to tell Harpocrates from Hephaestus, but it *will* be possible to drink in the embryo of the higher self with eyes like a liquid sun, up above the world so high, like a mirror in the sky.

BEN "drink to me only with thine eyes" Jonson wrote *News from the New World Discovered in the Moon*, a masque that was first performed in 1620, just after the very first English-language newspapers had been born. The masque reflected on new frontiers in astronomy and journalism, taking the explorer on a lunar journey and dropping him on the shores of the green world of paparazzi.

Through what he called a "trunk" (the object that would later be called a telescope), Jonson showed us the news today, oh boy, about a race of lunar birdmen called Volatees:

HERALD 2: Certain and sure news.

HERALD 1: Of a new world.

HERALD 2: And new creatures in that world.

HERALD 1: In the orb of the moon.

HERALD 2: Which is now found to be an earth inhabited.

HERALD 1: With navigable seas and rivers.

*Suggestions of violence and insanity...*

FACTOR: A fine lunatic language!

*Actors rush about claiming that the sun is getting bigger, the plague has broken out, there is thunder without lightning, etc.*

NARRATOR: And I saw when the Lamb opened one of the seals, and I heard, as it were the noise of thunder, one of the four beasts saying 'Shit!', then 'Piss!', then 'Fuck!', then 'Cunt!', then 'Cocksucker!' and then 'Motherfucker!'

And I beheld when he had opened the sixth seal, and, lo, there was a great earthquake; and the sun became black as sackcloth of hair, and the moon became as blood.

*A group of scientists appear and disagree with each other vehemently about what is happening while a Revolutionary objects: 'It isn't science anymore, it's immoral.' Another promises us, not very reassuringly, 'We won't see the antichrist yet.'*

*Finally, a scientist comes forth to the audience and shouts: 'Tits!'*

FACTOR: Aaaaaaaaarrrrrgggggghhhhhhhh!

HERALD 2: STUPENDOUS DISCOVERY!

HERALD 1: Of a new world.

$\mathcal{B}$EYOND fear, there is another world. On the other side of the curtain, beyond the dread of crashing and burning in a production of *The Frozen Deep*, there is a new life of unearthly beauty and others that we know not of.

The lamb will lie down with the lion, and the talons of the owl will be welcomed by the creature whose heart is pierced by them because when the beating drum of the lonely heart is sliced in two by a mirror, the truth is revealed...

*Through the Diana Dors, towards the Shirley Temple, the image of the egg-headed alien, Will-Lam Campbell or Billy ShakeShears, is pulled out of a famous record sleeve in a symbolic musick act.*

The starling that was taught to say 'Mortimer' delivers the message of death by love, the weakness for your destroyer that carries you across the void of senseless existence and senseless nonexistence to the place where it never happened for a reason, to the shores of the undiscovered country.

What seemed like a black abyss is the sea of ink in which every alien pen is dipped to write the tragedies so newspaper taxis can take you away. 'Forgive me for what I've done, I could not resist love...'

Owls prey on other birds as well as insects and even dogs, the latter seeming especially appetising between July 23 and August 23 of every year. When they want to eat Beatles, the birds will use dung as a form of bait to entice the Quarrymen underground, into a Cavern Club, where they are forced to perform sacrificial musick acts spelled out by the biorhythmic sheet music. The walls are smeared with shit and the food safety standards are broken like an eggshell seal in the nest of the earth, but the punishment is a strange kind of knowledge...

*You could not, would not and never were.*
*And what crime is that?*
'She loves you, yeah, yeah, yeah...'
*You are forgiven.*

84

HE Volatees, the race of lunar birdmen in Jonson's *News from the New World Discovered in the Moon,* derive from Lucian of Samosata's *True History*, about a group of sailing adventurers who are blown so far off course that they end up on the Moon and are caught up in a war between the lunar and solar kings over the colonisation of the Morning Star. Lucian also describes a race of beings from Sirius, called the Cynobalani, who had the bodies of men and the heads of dogs, much like the Egyptian god Anubis, and who rode upon winged acorns.

Once again, the food safety standards are broken because, just like the owl, which symbolises wisdom, acorns, the symbols of knowledge, are extremely dangerous and potentially fatal to dogs.

'Hey, is that an oak tree?' I asked the carman in front.

He pulled up his collar and shrugged.

ITH darkness turning on the table and the shittr sinking behind the trees, it seemed like the perfect moment to carry out one final piece of research, to drop a pine needle in a new life and become a wise eco-reader before flying off to the sunnymoon suite in the hotel at the end of time.

As the stars above alluded brightly to their unbearable reality, I stepped out of the forest and was blown into town, where I found a couple of human guinea pigs who, after an evening of drinking Guinness, were standing unsteadily in a kebab shop on Honor Oak Road.

To drop an at-om bomb at midnight, to put all wisdom down in writing, to become a university wit, perchance to gain a morsel of underground knowledge and realise that the mistaken belief about an owl's call being "twit twoo" derives from Shakespeare—ay, there's the post-pub grub, and in it I will slip a coiled-up myth that acts as an acasual connecting principle between twitterers on opposite sides of the Globe.

Shakespeare tried to make the overlapping owl calls fit rhythmically into a verse in *Love's Labour's Lost* while I took up a scientorial position against the counter in the temporary laboratory and began stridulating my heavenly instruments like shakespheres of dung at the two grtash test dummies waiting for their doners at the other end.

I pretended to be studying the menu as the humming increased. The two drunk men didn't realise what was going on, but I could see that the phenomenon was having a strong effect on them because their shirts were rippling and beads of sweat were rolling down their faces.

'Ummmmmmmmmmm...just a portion of chips, please,' I said at 100 wingbeats per second.

Man A leaned his head against the window and created a small waterfall of sweat which trickled all the way down to a shelf on which a newspaper had been placed: 62 Volatees waiting in the past to be taken across time and space; the owls of *Love's Labour's Lost* and the starlings of *Henry IV, Part 1* preparing to meet in the middle of the Globe like two dead lovers.

*When the peacock deploys its feathers, it can also make them hum at a level that competes with the traffic noise...*

Exactly as planned, the newspaper article about a tragedy and a scandal became soaking wet, collapsing human history into a soggy mess of words and images. John the Baptist was dunking Jesus in a river of sewage as a diesel truck rumbled past on its way to collide with Tara Browne in 1966...

A slowed-down recording of the scene later revealed that I had created a hideous piece of instrumental music at twice the speed of a hummingbeatle with a seemingly innocuous action. The sound described many years before by Charles Darwin, who once ate a brown owl during a meeting of the Glutton Society at Cambridge, was heard by the most perceptive members of the Yaudience in a slow-motion video of me scraping a wooden chip fork against a Styrofoam tray.

*T'wit-T'yaaaaauuuuuuuuuuuuuuuuuuuuuu...*

The screech was like a violin note which lasted a third of a second, a coiled-up false dawn chorus that embedded itself in the air at the end of 'A Day in the Life' like a flock of starlings in an Electra engine. Just as no one but the dogs could hear the bark of the tree falling in the nearby Calabi-Yau forest, the tone of the wooden tuning fork made from it was a highly specialised branch of knowledge, both human and divine, which was held only by a very small elite of underground university wit-to-woos despite its effects being clearly visible to all.

Man B then joined the first in leaning against the window. *Salmonella, burnt umbrella...a dirty watermarkfall from Paradise... Curiously Coloured After Life, with a Full and Accurate Description of Each*

*Figure, to which is Added A Brief and General Idea of Drawing and Paint-ing in Water-colours; with Instructions for Etching on Copper with Aqua Fortis.*

As both men fell into the drink, following *The Descent of Man* to its inverted climax, all that remained was for me to drop a bright green-gold hint in the acoustic niche of the chilli sauce so it would later be possible to distinguish between different species just by their hum. Food poisoning would be blamed for the vomiting and diarrhoea, and amid the sound and the fury, the "Lam of God in pitta bread" would travel to the altar of cruelty with the Lie-om and await the last syllable of recorded time at the height of the DogEnd Days.

OME birds don't have voices but are still able to produce music. Using bills, wings, tails, feet and feathers as instruments, they create non-vocal sounds that contain all sorts of messages.

Although existing body parts are usually utilised for this purpose, there are some instances where feathers are specially modified in order to produce what Charles Darwin called "instrumental music".

The bill of Thoth was often depicted as a writing instrument which gave Darwin the words with which to express himself.

'A fine lunatic language! They have leave only to HUM and HA.'

'Humans don't understand, do they?'

'No.'

'How I wonder what you are...'

I was walking through the forest and trampling the leaves of sheet music underfoot while humming the K-I-S-S-I-N-G song in an attempt to remember the lyrics, but the Apple of Knowledge remained on the tip of my love, Mother Tongue.

"The Hum" is an anomalous acoustic phenomenon reported in many countries across the world. People who can hear it complain of a persistent low-frequency humming sound like a distant diesel engine which can cause sickness, headaches and psychological distress.

The hums in different places around the world are often named after the location where they are heard, such as the Taos Hum, which began in the town of Taos in New Mexico 1991 and is still perceived to this day.

> He said he would not ransom Mortimer;
> Forbad my tongue to speak of Mortimer;
> But I will find him when he lies asleep,

And in his ear I'll holla 'Mortimer!'
Nay,
I'll have a *starling* shall be taught to speak
Nothing but 'Mortimer,' and give it him
To keep his anger still in motion.

'...the excitation of certain nervous centres causes physiological effects which are evoked by the utterance of certain letters or words which make no sense in themselves...'

'Mortimer, Mortimer, Mortimer... 62 people killed in 1960 by this one Shakespearean bword!'

Unfortunately the knowledge of how to construct a "word of power" is known by many governments across the world, and it is frequently used against the populace. The word most commonly used to oppress people is "YHWH", which can cause a huge range of physical and psychological symptoms, including sickness, headaches and delusions, when it is deployed.

A word of power can occupy a particular frequency and spread its influence laterally, giving those who only focus on one frequency the impression that they can hear "the truth" or "the voice of God".

Words of power are not inherently bad, however, and it is only their use by people with sinister intentions that results in negative effects. Many individuals are trying to fight back with words of opposition such as "buckarastano" and "grtash".

INTERROGATOR: Tell us!

SUSPECT: Aum.

INTERROGATOR: What the-?

SUSPECT: Calabi-Yauuuuuuuuuuuuuuuuuummmmmmmmmm.

INTERROGATOR: Aaaaaaaaaarrrrrgggggghhhhhhhh! Make it stop!

*I*n one of the pictures you can see two creatures sitting either side of the entrance to the Holiday Cavern. One creature has its mouth open while the other has its mouth closed; together they create the word Om. *Here, take a look at the Polaroid... you can actually* see *the sound of the word. It's shaped like a zero or an egg.*

This description is like a picture of a picture which allows you to peer through the leaves, to read between the wires in the library and foretell the weather.

*It's difficult to tell if it's a hotel or a tomb, a Life Building or a Death Building. It's arrived at by following a guiding star through the air or across the sea, I know that much. The customs officer will ask you if it's business or pleasure, to which it's best just to respond that it's a binary system, a mixed-media image including a photograph of a mirror and a whirlpool of dark paint in which a blue dot and its red-shifted twin are visible.*

Everyone has a Ramon and everytwo has a Paul, and from that mighty whirl of death, which takes us to the finyl act made from the blood of the Tarahumara Browne people, the myth of a lookalike is extracted: Amon-Ra is Ramon-A and CoulOm-B is Paul McCart-me.

As his passengers began sipping their black liquids, an inbound pilot above Boston Harbor in 1960 announced: 'Tower, an Electra just went into the drink!'

He was referring to an incident in which a Lockheed L-188 Electra aircraft setting off from Logan International Airport in Boston flew into a flock of starlings from Shakespeare's *Henry IV, Part 1* and crashed into Winthrop Bay, killing 62 people.

A final scene of cruelty was illuminated by the sun before it sank backstage like a shittr as volunteer rescuers waded through the mud and tried to help the victims. Most were dead and those who survived had swallowed oil and were critically ill.

'Collecting the corpses from the drink is a dirty job, but it really puts things into perspective, doesn't it?'

ow do you survive the dropping of the Atum bomb? How do you travel at 45 rpm from every track on the record, at 45 degrees from all four Beatles? The answer is hidden in the tragic news and needs to be sipped from the liquid wreckage...

According to the secret schools, Guinness heir Tara Browne first crashed the four-pedalled Lotus, then the six-pedalled Lotus, then the ten-pedalled Lotus, then the twelve-pedalled Lotus, then the sixteen-pedalled Lotus, then the ninety-six-pedalled Lotus, then the Lotus with one thousand pedals, at which point the false reality was shattered and his soul was catapulted through the windscreen and into a huge Paul of black ink that would be used to print the story of his death. Within minutes, newspaper taxis with lights flashing and sirens wailing appeared on the shore of the world of paparazzi to take the crash victim away and turn him into a tragic star immortalised in the song 'A Day in the Life' by the Beatles.

Such creative retellings correspond to a magnum opus unfolding its bright petals in the Field of Reads and offering a colourful account of its origin as a seed sown in the black sludge of existence, where it spent years vibrating to the hum of the Lotus engine and inching up slowly towards the headlamps of the carwreck in order to receive illumination by seeing itself reflected as life itself in the surface of the Pool of Death. When the sailors return safely to the city, the pint of Guinness they raise in the pubs to the Liver Birds to celebrate is the portal through which their 7/4 steps in the endless abyssidian mirror of space will be retraced.

When one journey has finished, another begins, but the hum of the engine will continue forever as a slowed-down recording of the screeching birds or the screeching brakes in the tiny coiled-up moment before death which functions as the run-out groove of this reality.

Just like Ben *"Mortimer His Fall"* Jonson, I saw the news to-day:

62 PEOPLE KILLED IN PLANE CRASH CAUSED BY BIRD STRIKE

The flock of around 20,000 starlings involved in the crash flew out of the works of Shakespeare, following a trail of sparkling breadcrumbs straight into the path of the Electra aircraft.

Starlings are not native to North America and were introduced by Eugene Schieffelin, a man whose aim was to make New York's Central Park a home to all the songbirds mentioned in the Bard of Avon's writings. The starlings spread across the continent like words of power, often at the expense of many native bwords, and had a negative effect on both the US economy and the ecosystem.

According to Socrates, a soul has to suffer being blown about for 10,000 years, in all directions on the compass and even into the engines of aeroplanes, before it becomes strong enough to fly back to its star nest, and there is no telling what the wind will blow through the psychoanalyst's window next.

MANY people enjoy the music produced by the wind when it uses telegraph wires as instruments, but some people claim it also has a practical use: to foretell the weather.

When the "songs of the wires" consist of high tones such as *Yau*, snow can be expected, while lower humming tones such as *Om* denote rain.

The weather was good the whole time I was on holiday, as you can see from the pictures. We travelled an incredibly long way through the ruins and the woods, but it was worth it.

'It's singing the light into existence!'

'Yes,' said the professor. 'Yes, it is.'

My companion's headlamp glowed warmly and for once there was no doubt in my mind. The wires mapped out the path the energy took through the mind of the receiver of the message. The birds sitting on the cables opened their beaks in amazement and let the fruit fall to the ground, seeding the earth with a splat.

'I've seen the future and it has seen me. I am the twinkle in the eye!'

Some people flip the idea on its head and claim the weather predicts the songs of the wires, but the more astute among us realise that the songs and weather are one and the same thing. Saying one exists to announce the arrival of the other is like saying the left hand is a sign of the clapping of the right hand.

At this point, the professor and I, "onely with a twofold difference", stopped to applaud an act on a higher stage. We looked up at Bizet's *Kármán* vortex sheet music and discovered there was only ever one bird on the Lockheed L-188 Electra wires.

HERALD 2: They do all in clouds there; they walk i' the clouds, they sit i' the clouds, they lie i' the clouds, they ride and tumble i' the clouds, their very coaches are clouds.

PRINTER: But ha' they no carmen to meet and break their coaches, to collect the corpses from the drink?

HERALD 2: Alas, carmen! They will over a carman there, as he will do a child here, you shall have a coachman with cheeks like a trumpter, and a wind in his mouth, blow him afore him as far as he can see him; or skirr over him with his bat's wings a mile and a half ere he can steer his wry neck to look where he is.

*K*ármán tells the story of the soldier who is seduced by a gypsy woman. The soldier has his life destroyed by the swirling pattern of vortices known as Kármán and ends up murdering her in a jealous rage.

Looking down from the wires or the clouds, it is possible to read a report in the newspaper landscape that refers to the cause of the murder as a 'stroke of apoplexy,' but the view from the highest position of all reveals that the experience was just an operatic illusion created by Neferkaptah, which presents Don José with a choice between returning the libretto to the tomb in fear, or transcending himself in order to be able to assimilate the information.

126 years after Baroness Mary Vetsera's death, her farewell letters were discovered in a bank vault in Vienna.

'Please forgive me for what I've done, I could not resist love... I want to be buried next to Him in the Cemetery of Alland. I am happier in death than life.'

The letters were found inside an envelope sealed with the Crown Prince Rudolf's insignia; they passed through a passage of time in the vault and hatched into a blue bird. The mystery of the deaths is still unsolved, but the mystery of death itself isn't, which changes everything...

*I broke the seal of the bread and read the message with a smile. Whatever survives the destruction of the envelope, the burning of the flesh umbrella, can dance canary with spritely fire and motion up to the higher branches, where it is reunited.*

*Reunited with what?*

*Just reunited.*

You could not have killed your lover because she was never real. You were never real either. You were written by Henri Meilhac and Ludovic Halévy, who based you on a novella by Prosper Mérimée. You were first performed at the Opéra-Comique in Paris, on March 3rd 1875, lasting almost three hours, but you weren't particularly successful.

A PARTIAL eclipse of the Moon occurs on Saturday 23 February, 2464 UT, with maximum eclipse at 10:50 UT. The Moon will be strikingly shadowed in this deep partial eclipse lasting two hours and 58 minutes, with 73% of the Moon in darkness at maximum.

I travelled to the other side of the Globe to test the hypothesis that man is just a Hum-on being, a vibratory entity with an eternally urgent question flapping its wings in his throat. If the humming were ever to stop, the human would stop.

INTERROGATOR: Aaaaaaaaarrrrrgggggghhhhhhhh! Make it stop!

During a solar eclipse, the birds will fall silent. As the black disc is pushed along London Road and up Taymount Rise to the top of the sky charts, the music seems to stop, but it is in fact the most dramatic musical production of all because silence is golden.

All the creatures on earth fall silent out of respect for the full stop. The universe offers a rare glimpse into the closed circle of Author, Character and Reader, and meaning itself becomes visible.

When the punctuation mark has passed, the audible communication of the birds is recommenced and a false dawn chorus is performed for the audience members.

I am standing in an editorial position on the bank of the river, watching the miracle in awe. Dark is the sky and bright are the stars that shine, and I know all this travelling of mine has been worth it.

The second dawn in the space of a day appears and becomes the seal of approval for the many years of single sunrises which saw me flying sol-o around the Globe in the mothership and chasing a vital piece of information in order to crack the in-eggma code.

When you can no longer recognise your papamummy,

birth and death are conjoined twins, and a sense of closure is an opening night of dayseals in the Skull Theatre, trepanned by critics and praised to high heaven by Jesus and a pelican as words are used as blunt instruments against the divided but enantiomorphic audience.

*Grtash!*

*The red rock at the entrance of the tomb rolls away...*

*Wandering on the banks of your water and resting in the shadow of your sycamore, the suffering is no more. All the major playhouses you planted can now be seen: the Globe, the Swan, the Rose, the Hope. This singularity is the "final beginning" signposted by almost all of the DMRI's experiments.*

A N eclipse was frequently described as the sun being devoured by a serpent, and in many ancient societies, people would try to make as much noise as possible by banging objects together to scare the giant serpent or dragon away during an eclipse.

'Aaaaaaaaarrrrrgggggghhhhhhhh! Mortimer, Mortimer, Mortimer!'

The leaves were rustling a Scarab Beatles tune for me, and I suddenly understood it: I am the eggmanifold, they are the eggmenifold; the microcosm and the macrocosm. The material world was about to devour the sun like a snake swallowing an egg but, just in time, I cracked the genomic safeword with my tongue, clicking through all possible readings of 'A Day in the Life' in the pix-cell to reveal the meta meaning hidden in The End.

'You've shattered everything.'

The word "SCARAB" is linked to the word "SCRIBE" via Synthetic Cellular Recorders Integrating Biological Events, which explains why the Beatles wrote so much sheet music.

Thoth, the scribe of the gods, would accompany Ra on his voyage on the solar boat. At night, when the gods attempted to travel from east to west via a river through the underworld, the barge would be attacked by a huge serpent called Apep in the dark waters below.

According to myth, the god Ra carried the sun across the heavens on a mystical solar boat every day; every evening, Ra returned from west to east via an unseen river path through the underworld. As night covered the world and the sun god laboured to return to the farthest point in the east in time for sunrise, the great serpent would appear from the dark waters to attack the boat.

People in Egypt would "worship against" Apep by creating images of the beast that were spat at, hit with sticks and eventually destroyed.

'Sally?'

'Yes, dear Betty?'

'If I died, would you be sad?'

'Of course! I'd be devastated.'

'Would you rush out and burn the sacred circle of trees to a black disc?'

'Probably.'

'Then I'd like you to promise me something...'

'OK.'

'If I die, you need to return to the asylum and destroy something for me. It's a painting of a dark river which you'll find on the wall of one of the art rooms. It's my work, but it was painted with poison, a poison called "flesh". I think it started off as a salmon but it grew darker and darker the more the sun shone on it, until it became a black snake, then a contaminated river and the shadow of the sun's path. Will you destroy it for me? It's extremely dangerous.'

'I promise to destroy the snake for you.'

'Thanksss.'

The rare days that were overcast or stormy were interpreted as the result of Apep gaining superiority over Ra. The low hum of the wires of the pylon denoted rain, and the two creatures, one with its mouth open and the other with its mouth closed, formed the word *Om*, creating and destroying the city of Liverpool in one fell swoop.

The monumental gateway to an Egyptian temple, known as a pylon, echoed the hieroglyph for "horizon", which represented two hills behind which the sun rose and set. We now know that the underworld is just the other side of the globe and that the sun is never swallowed by Apep. Backstage at the Globe Theatre, the star of *Summers Last Will* is shining brightly...

When the gold-green-brown egg passes through the trapdoor in the trapdoor and pops out of Mother Theatre, beginning and end can both be wiped with the 7/4 sheet music of the Dung Beatles.

'Don't worry,' said Beatle A. 'You can sing your "onely" little heart out without fear of being understood by the narrow-minded. That's because anything can be made to signify anything thanks to the Biliteral Bacon and Egg Cipher, whose creator said: "For by this Art a Way is opened, whereby a man may expresse and signifie the intentions of his minde, at any distance of place, by objects which may be presented to the eye, and accommodated to the eare: provided those objects be capable of a twofold difference onely; as by Bells, by Trumpets, by Lights and Torches, by the report of Muskets, and any instruments of like nature." The power to "signifie omnia per omnia" is no less than the power of divine om-nificence!'

'Yes,' said Beatle B. 'A twofold difference onely. Let's do it at the double!'

Bishop John Wilkins, author of *The Discovery of a World in the Moone* and proponent of a new universal language, was an important figure in the history of cryptography. He recommended writing with raw egg as a way of keeping the contents of letters hidden, and also detailed a musical cipher so that anyone familiar with it could "easily discern how two Musicians may discourse with one another by playing upon their Instruments of Musick as well as by talking with their Instruments of Speech."

A great secret and a multitude of hidden characters can be brought into the light...

THE Scarab Beatles remain one of the most remarkable symbolic musick acts ever conceived by the mind of man. They were first discovered in a cavern in Liverpool by renowned entomologist Brian Epstein, who saw in their peculiar habits and appearance the chance to represent the mysteries of the cosmos to humankind.

Over the course of a decade, the Scarab Beatles evolved from a group of simple insects into universal symbols, attracting millions of worshippers among both the vulgar masses and the privileged priesthood.

In the 1960s, people believed that the sky was a huge music chart up which a giant Beatle rock-and-rolled a circular piece of vinyl. When the disc was at the top of the hit parade, it was said to turn from black vinyl into solid gold and reflect the light of fame back down to earth for the glory of all music fans.

There is a secret chamber of the heart in which the Scarab Beatles can be heard playing music with unusual spacetime signatures, the expression of the true self streaming over the airwaves of the undiscovered country.

The darkest moment in Jesus' life was when he was under the burning sun, asking why he had been forsaken; similarly, the Dung Beatles had to break the seal of the morning and stir the black sun of coffee to earn their wings.

*Did Ramon ever exist separately from me?*

Because the Fab Four wings unfolded suddenly from the body of the 1960s, displaying their psychedelic colours and transcending the gloom of the previous era, the Scarab Beatles were the creatures best suited to publicly bouncing the rubber soul. Thanks to earlier hints such as Aleister Crowley's Thelemic Hearts Club Band and the Yellow Submarine Solar Boat, initiates knew that the Abbey Road crossing would end in rebirth rather than death.

The run-out groove leads to the Apple of Eden, and all four

parts of the group are reunited to perform *Free as a Bird* despite two of them, Paul and John, being "dead".

The water is poisoned and the air is thin. I think I'll just sit down at the foot of this tree and read *Lucky Starr and the Ringos of Saturn* in silence...

ICHARD Dadd, who is famous for both painting and patricide, began showing signs of mental disturbance in 1842 while in the Holy Land with Sir Thomas Phillips, a wealthy patron for whom Dadd was meant to produce drawings and watercolours. Dadd's symptoms were dismissed as sunstroke, but after being sent home, the artist stabbed his father to death and was confined to Bethlem Hospital.

The sights of the Orient were mixed in with the morning coffee and re-imagined as the stuff of nightmares. Shakespearean scenes with the eyes turned inwards, a raving figure from the 1850s in a chilling self-reference.

*It's a painting of a black snake in heavy ink on the wall of the asylum. It needs to be broken down into breadcrumbs. It needs to pine for me in a new life.*

The artist's waters had been poisoned, which meant the snake was able to rise up in an E. coli self-portrait and devour him as he attempted to journey from west to east. Walking up Taymount Rise and dropping breadcrumbs that he could not perceive, an Englishman left that curious 19th-century genre in ruins.

*To survive the illusion is to destroy it.*

Archduke Karl Ludwig, the father of Archduke Franz Ferdinand of Austria, died in 1896 due to an infection picked up by drinking water in the Holy Land.

*Paradisaea rudolphi*, the scientific name of the blue bird-of-paradise, commemorates the Crown Prince Rudolf of Austria, whose father had no other children.

*Diadophis punctatus edwardsii*, a subspecies of North American snake, is named in honour of George Edwards, the "father of British ornithology".

Ornithology is a branch of zoology that concerns the study of birds. Etymologically, the word "ornithology" derives from the ancient Greek *ornis* ("bird") and *logos* ("rationale" or "explanation").

Egyptian scripts could be seen as one of the earliest forms of ornithology as they function as records of the birds seen in the area at the time. Individual species can be recognised in the hieroglyphs.

In 1901, in the introduction to *The Birds of North and Middle America*, Robert Ridgway wrote:

> There are two essentially different kinds of ornithology: systematic or scientific, and popular. The former deals with the structure and classification of birds, their synonymies and technical descriptions. The latter treats of their habits, songs, nesting, and other facts pertaining to their life histories.

*Perhaps my life story is a text in an E. colibrary within the body of a higher being. Perhaps I was killed by swallowing someone else's life story.*

I had obtained the piece of information I had been searching for: the story of my death.

'This is it, old chap,' said Ramon solemnly. 'You ready?'

'Ready as I'll ever be.'

As the wise old professor turned to wood, I looked up and read the message in the stars:

> There are two essentially different kinds of you: the mortal and the immortal. My love for you pertains to the latter. Good luck in getting where you need to go.
>
> —Love Polly, your sweetheart.

I looked up through the hole eaten in the paralune by the acausal connecting principle to see a giant metallic bird carrying me like a human letter to my destination. It was night, and there was no turning back. I had to make one last flight, to the other side of the Globe, to the Unholy Land...

ANUBIS is associated with the mummification and protection of the dead for their journeys through Denver International Airport to the afterlife. He is usually portrayed as being half human and half jackal, and holding a metal detector in his hand. The distinctive colour of Anubis' uniform is associated with everything that is rotten in the US state of Colorado. Anubis is employed by the Department of Homeland Security to examine the hearts of all travellers to make sure they have not exceeded the weight limit for psychological baggage.

Anubis is sometimes depicted performing other tasks related to customs and excise. In addition to checking luggage, he is also shown frisking mummies and confiscating firearms and other contraband. It doesn't take much to tip the scales in favour of a dead body cavity search or an afterlifetime travel ban.

When I arrived at Denver International Airport, the light and sound were both ominously low, and the air was so thin I could barely breathe. I told myself the darkness and silence were in anticipation of a second dawn in one day, but in my heart, which was now beating wildly on my sleeve, there was no certainty. I looked around the secret bunker for trees to help me breathe, but there were none.

Panting like a Beatle pushing a boulder up the final stage, I approached Anubis, who was waiting at the scanner and aiming an icy stare in my direction like Big Trouble in Little Colorado. I had no choice but to proceed towards him in the hope of being permitted to board the afterdeath plane.

'Please take off your tweed jacket and step through the Scanner of Justice,' Anubis said in a deep voice.

I tried to make a joke about him being assigned the job of "Guardian of the Scanner" due to someone mistaking the word "god" for "guard" when pronounced with an American accent, but the jackal-headed airport employee didn't show any sign of amusement.

'Insert Sirius pun here,' I muttered.

'Just step through the scanner, please sir.'

I glanced nervously at the two-way mirror, behind which a hungry Ammit was probably licking her crocodile lips in anticipating of a human om nom nom nomelette, before following Anubis' orders and hoping for the best.

'Everybody's got something to hide except for me and McCartney,' I whispered hopefully to myself.

*Grtash!*

As my heart was examined, a flash of lightning illuminated the tree of my life, making all the branches and arteries visible at once. The bright bolt was a pinprick from death and a Lifepak in a new world which caused the tree to split apart and shed its skin before me. The way forward was now carpeted with leaves from my life story, which would be trodden into oblivion as I proceeded through the Hall of Ma'at. The record of my life was a map through death. The layers of peeling bark were unfurling scrolls of charred skin on which *Beneath the Burnt Umbrella* had been written in egg.

'The airport has been blown up by lightning,' a voice announced over the airwaves. 'It happens from time to time.'

*But how am I going to travel now?* I thought to myself in a moment of panic.

'Just board the afterdeath plane,' the voice replied, seemingly able to hear my thoughts.

*But surely that's not possible if the airport's been blown up! Something's gone horribly wrong!*

'No, old chap, it's gone horribly right. The explosion is how you board the plane, how you travel, how you see the stars. Look...'

I released the eye from the jar and saw *The Story of the First Ever Human Being to be Saved by the Loving Feather of Everything* in the sky. It had been written by A Rastano using the bill of Thoth. The description of the quill is not the quill, but if it is written by the quill, then the raven is the writing desk and meaning itself is visible.

'I see what you mean.'

'Oh Annie! Polly! Polly-Anne!'

'You made it, my love!'

'But how?'

'A feathered friend, a member of the Birdon race, silently took on your burden so you would be light enough to pass through the nowhere-port. A shadow heart beat soundlessly so you didn't suffer occult heart failure. And now we have nothing to declare but our love!'

'She loves you, yeah, yeah, yeah...'

With our eyes fully open, we stared at each other from the ends of time to do our bit for universal symbols. Wings sprouted from the sides of the deathbed and we were away, high above the smouldering wreckage of the silver aeroplane, above society's superficial descriptions of a scandal and a tragedy. World of paparazzi—that small carousel on which the Guinness heir collides with a diesel truck and dies of his injuries.

The newspapers said: 'Say, what you doing in bed?'

I said: 'We're only trying to get us some peace.'

In 'The Singular Affair of the Baconian Cipher,' Sherlock Holmes reads a hidden message in the morning newspaper, which takes him to Penge—along Honor Oak Road, a Holmes is just a Watson travelling backwards in time, up Taymount Rise to the apparent "dead end" which is in fact a circular entrance to the boundless centre of the action; in and out and up and away, the roots of the Tree of Life finally unclenching with a profound sense of opening-closure.

Annie was Polly and she and I were every young couple in love. From high above that place they call the universe, we could see our shadows in their entirety for the first time; we could take possession of them but they no longer tied us to the earth because, through the hole punctured in the parasol by the beetle of synchronicity, that green girl and I spied each other safely home. All's well that ends well in our burning love for the warm sun and the beginning of the post-temporal honeymoon period, nowhere out in inner space together, on the motherbarque.

We had passed from the realm of unreal nonfiction to real fiction. We were in the Field of Reads, the Infinite Library, a place where all the stories you collect during your life unwind into the air you breathe.

We took a look around and found everything we were looking for, including a book called *The True Story of Baucis and Philemon*, which told the story of two gods who pretended, for the benefit of Zeus and Hermes, not to be divine and were then turned into intertwined linden and oak trees that grew from the seeds of love planted in death.

We also found, in a lime and acorn sandwich, a story called 'Oh Time Thy Pyramids.'

Borges said, 'I have always imagined that Paradise will be a kind of library,' so someone will understand the importance of this...

Oh Time Thy Pyramids by Buck Arastano

Buck A Rastano is an enlightened author who introduces metafictional writing techniques to the Egyptians. A rival writer called Set, who specialised in linear murder mystery stories, finds his book sales are adversely affected by the popularity of Buck, so he decides to plot the real-life murder of his literary competitor.

Set invites Buck to a book reading and shows his rival a richly decorated book that he says has been made especially for him as it contains the life story of Buck A Rastano. As the metafictional author is peering inside the book, Set slams it shut, trapping him inside the text, which turns out to be a prophetic account about one writer trapping another writer inside a murder story.

The jealous but triumphant murder writer seals the book and throws it into the marketplace, where it is eventually picked up by Malacander, the King of Biblos, who gives it pride of place in his great library.

Annie Rastano, the wife of Buck, searches for her husband high and low, in all the bookshops and libraries in the world, until she finally locates him in Biblos. She takes him back to Egypt and tries to conceive of a sequel or a new edition of his life story that has a happy ending, but Set finds out what has happened and splits the book up into 14 separate chapters which are then scattered across the land so the denouement cannot be reached.

Annie, along with the help of Thoth and Anubis, gathers up all but one of the chapters and binds them together in a leather book. Only the sex scene, which was swallowed up by a censor, is missing from the volume, so Annie pens a new one consisting of double entendres alluding to the act of lovemaking in which their brainchild, a metafictional magnum opus called *Buck II*, is conceived.

Set's attempts to suppress Buck's metafictional works were always doomed to failure because he could not carry them out without adding to the metafiction. Transcending the self is the ultimate form of self-protection, and a meta murder is always a rebirth on a higher level. The tragedy is *within* the story, but it is also what allows the couple to escape from the book and look down on it from a glorious editorial position.

*Buck II* continues the story of *Buck I*, and the tomb is revealed to be a cleverly disguised bookwormhole. The ultimate murder mystery is an investigation of the mystery of death itself, which is solved when it is revealed to be a meta mystery without an end, my dear Watson.

HE birds and the trees missing from the story of Buck A Rastano can be found in the so-called real world, where terrible secrets are also located. The first book we perceive will spontaneously combust and the bird will return to the smouldering wreckage each evening.

After the disappearance of Stephen Moles, the authorities raid the Dark Meaning Research Institute's liboratory and seize all the organisation's books and papers in the hope of possessing the profound secret that has been undermining their work for so long. What they fail to realise, however, is that if they are not worthy of it, *the secret will possess them...*

Soon after the raid, the grand narrators begin to feel like they have swallowed sewage from the Holy Land. The stomach cramps kick in, followed by vomiting and diarrhoea, and then a series of terrifying hallucinations which make them want to return the documents to the tomb and beg Thoth for forgiveness.

The effect of the knowledge depends on what it is affecting. To those who can contain it, it is an Ecolibrary; to the bad eggs it is a potentially deadly infection.

The Privy Council discover polysemy the hard way when "privy" turns out to also mean "toilet" and they are forced to eat their own dirty words. The Meaning Police, who try to enforce a single way of behaving and thinking, are overwhelmed by the force of multiple meanings as Poley and Parrot come home to roost.

The police can easily be made to police the police because one cleverly crafted word of power can eclipse them completely.

'You mean everything to me,' I told the object of my love.

"ᴀʏ I walk every day unceasing on the banks of my water; may my soul rest on the branches of the trees which I have planted; may I refresh myself in the shadow of my sycamore."

You can travel around the world and try to see every solar eclipse, but you can also travel around to do the opposite and remain in the light, turning black in the heat of an endless day if moving at the right speed and in the right direction. The sun repeatedly rises in the east from the point of view of those who sit still and await its return at that point, but from another perspective it is forever moving west, further and further away from its starting point, while from yet another position it is not moving at all. The sun never really rises or sets; we just turn to face it or turn our back on it.

Night is a necessary event, but it can be experienced in all sorts of Ways, including by dunking the sun into the morning coffee like a biscuit. Death is just the body in its own shadow, and the hole in the parasol leads back to the green language, the beetle lyrics eaten into the first leaf on the Tree of Meaning, the beautiful birdgirl, my love, Mother Tongue.

All of my tomorrows came at once and I found myself over-standing the umbrella of human skin which was turning from pink to amber to burnt umber to smoking black beneath my gaze: all flesh is a parasol that blocks out the light, but the longer it remains there, the darker it gets; and the darker it gets, the closer it is to having a hole burnt through it by the sun.

To be created, you must first be destroyed; ashes to ashes, The Way to dusty death. To dance canary with spritely fire, you must first withdraw from the external world and swim in the Pool of Darkness.

I could see the throne of Osiris resting on the surface of the black coffee like a lotus flower, but if I looked at it differently it could have been a soggy piece of newspaper depicting a crashed Lotus Elan floating in a pint of Guinness, or maybe even a river of sewage sweeping the stolen documents back to the tomb of Thoth.

I found myself moving across the surface of the thick black liquid like a swan on the grooves of a record; but after numerous spins on the turntable I realised I needed to find a way of breaking the cycle, so I looked up into the sky for navigational guidance and saw a bright white light like a headlamp of a car or a professor, like the heart of a Great Bird, a firework frozen in the moment of its explosion; then I could see the substance that previously appeared black, its oily surface now covered with iridescent colours and patterns swirling like the peacock's tail.

The turning point was the realisation that the Fall of Man was a fall *out* from the inner world rather than a fall *down* from Heaven, and this turning point was at right angles from all points in spacetime. I was able to take flight down the run-out groove and pursue a run-*in* with the zero-point of my life story.

**W**HY so many stories? Was this another layer of text or was it my actual experience?

I was in the Field of Reads, an Ecolibrary of my own making, where the *eBook of the Dead* opened up and offered me the premise of the *real fiction*, an egg I had nourished with the pain of carrying it around inside me.

Many humans, through no fault of their own, are forced to carry terrible secrets around inside them. A person can be forced into becoming the custodian of the memory of an atrocity committed by a god for the rest of its days simply by being in the wrong place at the wrong time.

A human who climbs to the top of a mountain may witness the massacre of an entire town below due to a fit of rage by YHWH. While the god wakes up the next day with a hangover and confusion about why there are burnmarks on his hands, the poor mortal spectator suffers intense recurring nightmares about the incident for the rest of his or her life, as if a bird from the black abyss whispered 'Mortimer' over and over again in their ear.

A human at the foot of a mountain may see Hephaestus, the child of Zeus and Hera, falling to earth and suffering serious injuries resulting in permanent disability. The human witness to the crime, seeing that Hephaestus was thrown off the peak by his own father as punishment for trying to protect his mother, will have to sit on the knowledge and hope that a plot for revenge does not hatch out.

What can those creatures with their infamously tiny attention spans teach us?

Quite a lot, as it happens.

The humans who take on the knowledge of the gods' darkest deeds are guaranteed to suffer in some way, but the very strongest among them endure the pain instead of rushing back to the tomb to return the magnum opus in fear. Surviving the illusion is a way of destroying it, so the night mirror tears your heart *open* rather than *apart*, and you emerge from the shell of the simulation in the centre of whatever it is that creates the shade of the mortal parasol with its light.

And whatever that is, it's not a "god".

Through his research, Stephen Moles discovered that humans are to gods what birds are to humans. We sit on divine secrets so that the gods can be gods, but that means we are above what we sit on. What we call mythology is one giant egg and to those outside it, every non-human large and small, its contents are a total mystery.

'Wait a Dogon minute!' barks the customs officer. 'Someone smuggled an egg through? What the—?'

I had managed to sneak the Beatles bootlegg across the border, past Anubis and Ammit, and into the undiscovered country, where it became that non-local territory's buried treasure, ensconced in a human chest deep inside the red earth.

A cross marked the spot from which the parasol with the ribs of Adam unfolded into the breast of the green girl, a multipara-lune that fed four sets of Siamese embryellas—John, Paul, Rise and Fall, along with their shadow hearts backing band—as they spun out at 45 rpm from the axis of the Globe Theatre.

The contra-band couldn't be detected by Anubis because it was formed from the secrets of the gods, the material that allows humans to fly to others that the deities know not of. It is possible for the secrets of the gods to be kept secret from the gods, for the mysteries to be watched over as mysteries rather than hidden away as knowledge, and for the heart 'To Have Done with the Judgment of God' via a concealed trapdoor that leads to itself.

As my heart unfolded in the spotlight of pure perception like a foetus emerging from the wreckage of a crashed Lotus or Electra, I finally saw the sound of the sacred utterance in the holiday snap as a self-singing hymnsheet, and I tasted the words that had been stuck on the tip of my tongue for so long... *smoked salmon umbrella; burnt umber, salmonella*. To those who can contain it, it is an infinite Ecolibrary; to the bad eggs it is a case of deadly food poisoning while overseas.

'They are the eggmen, I am the bwordman, a great way to begin and end the day.'

The lyrics of the playground song grew up and became the music of the self...

'First and Last sitting in a tree D-I-V-I-N-I-Tee. *And I love her.*'

The moment the chamber of the heart cracks open and you hear 'A Day In *Your* Life' is also the moment that the hood of the baby carriage comes down and the most pathetic sight imaginable is beheld. God's dirty little secret is that he needs you to feed him, clean him, nurture him, and redeem him.

That most wretched substance, from which alchemical gold can be produced, is almost never identified or obtained, not because people don't value it, but because they *overvalue* it, believing it to be already perfected and consequently not something they are worthy of possessing or even contemplating. It is thrown away for being *too valuable*.

Paradoxically, if we inspect it, we not only reveal its hidden wretchedness but also discover that that wretchedness is a product of our age-old refusal to process the substance.

It should be clear that the person who swallows excrement in a river in the Holy Land is no different from the person who manufactures genius in a shithole of a home on the other side of the world, and that divinity is the most basic substance there is.

The most wretched thing of all is only so wretched because it is treated as unimaginable—that is, *not treated*—which is like labelling the water of life "unimaginably pure" and believing that to be a form of refinement when it actually means "unprocessed by the imagination" and is therefore equivalent to "unimaginably filthy". When treated as *imaginable*, however, the most wretched substance is contained by *The Complete Sewage Works* and instantly finds itself in the process of being perfected.

Imperfection is the raw material from which perfection is made, and the most wretched substance *imaginable* is the qualitative opposite of the most wretched substance *unimaginable*.

Eggman, birdman, godman, poo...

You are what I wonder you.

'It's a dirty job, but someone's got to do it...' said Human A.

'We should get a god to help then,' replied Human B.

'Shhh! Not so loud, you tit! That's the *last* thing we should do!'

'Really? So what should we do?'

'We should keep quiet. Take a vow of silence.'

'Silence?' Human B replied, sounding miserable. 'But I'm a musician. I live for singing! I'd die if I had to keep this gift to myself.'

'Don't worry,' said the first human. 'You can still sing. In fact, that's the perfect way to both reveal and re-veil the gift. You can sing all the lonely hearts songs without fear of being understood by the censors, you can sneak all the supposedly dirty words through customs when your lips are sealed around a deafening gold disc of silence, and you can signify *every* single thing by *any* single thing to the Meaning Police. Got me?'

'Got you.'

*O M!*

When the upper orifice which expels the sacred word is wiped with the napkin of the newborn saviour, the biological sheet music that makes the Dung Beatles bigger than Jesus is composed. The reason I was warned not put the sacred word into writing was because it would look like a profanity, a streak of fuckshitpiss across the page, or a transcript of a stream of consciousness flowing from a giant pottymouth.

Arming himself with a notebook and pen, a researcher can explore the land and trace its features, including the giant fissures in the earth caused by the dropping of the at*om* b*om*b on the Globe's newspaper axis. When he fills in the deep cracks with ink from his pen, he is both mapping out and creating the scenery like a landscape painter with godlike delusions. *The alphabet of the stones, the syntax of the snakes...*

'It's a painting of a dark river that you'll find on the wall of the asylum. You must promise me you'll finish it off when I return to watery chaos at the end of the creative cycle, and that you'll make sure the music of the Liver Birds is played at my funeral. You promise you'll do this for me? It's very important.'

'Yes, I promise... and it's already done, no?'

'IF we use the secrets of humans to navigate, what do humans use?' asked Bird A.

'God knows,' replied Bird B.

It turns out that 'God knows' means 'no one but humans know' because what humans use to pass through funerary customs are the secrets of the customs officers, hidden away inside the egg of mythology—the best place to hide mythological secrets, just as the forest is the best place to hide a leaf.

A secret must be kept from the secret in order for the secret to know itself because the only place the secret's secret can be properly hidden is in its heart, as the trapstone on the zero-point, the end as the rolled beginning, the rediscovery of the green language on the tip of the Mother Tongue. If the secret survives the horror of discovering itself secreted in the tomb while taking part in a mythological eggman hunt, it can grow feathers of black vinyl and fly at right angles from all spatial directions as the Atum-bombshell splits apart like a false conception of the self and the egg hatches inwardly to a complex *"turn me on/in/over, deadmanifold"* in the combined first and last pages of the infinite e-book.

The way to escape the Theatre of Cruelty is to locate the new beginning hidden in the final scene, the tiny twinkle of pure white paper that remains unstained despite the grim bloodbath engulfing the end of the Shakespearean five-act structure. Safely tucked away inside the "terminal" act is a smaller sixth act which contains a smaller seventh act and so on; and inside each of those, one of the seven personalities that all play the fifth Beatle will step into the spotdark and shine, revealing finally and endlessly that the seven additional dimensions predicted by M-theory are to be found in the unexplored fifth cardinal direction. The Way Out is *In*.

*Ugh-ugh-ugh-ugh-ugh-ugh-ugh*—that strange vocalisation, incomplete yet without an end, which is etched into the tiny coiled-up run-out groove like a watermark in the Sgt Paper on which all life stories are written, is finally deciphered... *Shit, piss, fuck, cunt, cocksucker, motherfucker, tits! You wanker, you superman, you knew it all along.* It was made by moving at acceleran-gles of 45 rpm from every songline on the recorded landscape and following the high-pitched signal placed by John Lennon at the end of 'A Day in the Life' to make all the canines go crazy like it's the height of the Dog Days.

According to Xenophanes, Pythagoras believed in the transmigration of souls and interceded on behalf of a dog that was being beaten after claiming to recognise the cry of a de-parted friend inscribed on the bark of the animal: 'Yaaaauuu-uuuuuu!'

'Now, just wait a Dogon minute... How did you acquire knowledge of Sidereal B, the Twin-kle Mc-*ka*-tney on the flip-side of space, the vinyl frontier? You know binary star systems like Sirius have such a narrow habitable zone that the chances of life existing there are tiny, don't you?'

'Yes, but in this case, the narrower and tinier the better... the smaller the scale, the bigger the space for more dimen-sions. All you need is...'

'Love?'

'Either that or the 2464 matrix number etched into the run-out groove of reality by a diamond in the sky, yes.'

Up above the world so high, many people have wondered how the word "buckarastano" came into being—but it was their wonder that gave it life.

'You mean everything to me,' I told the object of my love... *and I meant it.* Polly was Annie and Elizabeth and Lucy and Ella and Juliet and Linda and Yoko because she was Polly. One lit-tle word is all you need if it's polysemous. It could be "love", "death", "buckarastano", "grtash" or even "nothing", just as long as Polly sees you in the sky with diamonds and makes the pure white feathers in the black duvet on the deathbed flutter excitedly.

'You've seen the...?'

'Yes.'

'Now we have nothing to declare but our love.'

I have seen a medicine that is able to breathe life into a stone, and that medicine has seen me. I love her more than anyone else in the world because she is everyone, and I love her and I love her and I love her.

*Author Photo by Fred Forse*

Stephen Moles is the author of seven books, including *Paul is Dead* (CCLaP) and *The More You Reject Me, the Bigger I Get* (Beard of Bees), as well as many other shorter pieces. He regularly carries out undercover literary assignments aimed at both fighting the centralisation of meaning and bringing about the linguistic singularity for the benefit of society. Stephen is also the founder of the Dark Meaning Research Institute, a group of parasemantic investigators and quantum linguistics pioneers who are currently working on a way to blast him off the page and turn him into the world's first zero-person author.

www.thedeathofstephenmoles.com